RSPCA

Animal Tales

The Four Paws Collection

Animal 🐕 Tales

THE FOUR PAWS COLLECTION

THE HAPPY TAILS COLLECTION

The Four Paws Collection

RANDOM HOUSE AUSTRALIA

A Random House book
Published by Random House Australia Pty Ltd
Level 3, 100 Pacific Highway, North Sydney NSW 2060
www.randomhouse.com.au

Ruby's Misadventure first published by Random House Australia in 2012
Lost in Translation first published by Random House Australia in 2012
A New Home for Cocoa first published by Random House Australia in 2012
Florence Takes the Lead first published by Random House Australia in 2012
This bindup edition first published by Random House Australia in 2013

Addresses for companies within the Random House Group can be found at
www.randomhouse.com.au/offices

National Library of Australia
Cataloguing-in-Publication Entry

Author: Kelly, Helen, 1969– .
Title: The four paws collection / Helen Kelly and David Harding.
ISBN: 978 0 85798 131 8 (paperback)
Series: RSPCA animal tales.
Target Audience: For primary school age.
Subjects: Cats – Juvenile fiction.
          Dogs – Juvenile fiction.
Other Authors/Contributors: Harding, David.
Dewey Number: A823.4

Cover photograph © imagestock / iStockphoto
Cover and internal design by Ingrid Kwong
Internal illustrations by Charlotte Whitby
Internal photographs: image of cat by iStockphoto, image of horse by Shutterstock,
image of dog by Patricia Doyle/Getty Images, image of horse © Lenkadan/Shutterstock
image of tick © ninjaMonkeyStudio/iStockphoto, image of Siberian kitten byDixi_/
iStockphoto, image of cat feeding by Rouzes/iStockphoto, image of British Shorthair by
Paul_Brighton/iStockphoto and image of pig by Tsekhmishter/iStockphoto
Typeset by Midland Typesetters, Australia
Printed in Australia by Griffin Press, an Accredited ISO AS/NZS 14001:2004
Environmental Management System printer.

Random House Australia uses papers that are natural, renewable and recyclable
products and made from wood grown in sustainable forests. The logging and
manufacturing processes are expected to conform to the environmental regulations of
the country of origin.

RSPCA

Animal Tales

Ruby's Misadventure

Ruby's Misadventure

Helen Kelly

RANDOM HOUSE AUSTRALIA

Chapter One

'Three sleepovers in a row! It's going to be just like we're sisters!' said Sarah.

Sarah was beside herself with excitement and Cassie let her go on without interruption. She was excited too, of course; it was going to be a wonderful few days.

School had finished and the girls were

passing by the park on their way home, just as they did every day. But today was different. Today was the day that they had both been looking forward to for weeks.

Sarah's parents had been married for eleven years and had decided that this year it was time for them to celebrate their wedding anniversary in style. They had booked themselves into a hotel on the beach for three whole days and children were not allowed!

'I still can't believe Mum let me stay here with you, instead of going to Gran's with the boys. It's going to be so quiet without them!' Sarah sighed. 'So, what shall we do first, Cassie? As my older and wiser *sister*, I think you should decide.'

'Mmmm. I am two months older and y'know, that really does make me very, very wise.' Cassie adopted her most thoughtful expression and pondered. 'How about starting with a milkshake?' This was a common suggestion from Cassie. Her mum and dad ran the local deli in Abbotts Hill and made the best milkshakes for miles around.

'Perfect!' agreed Sarah.

'Then we could take Ripper down to the park for a run. You know Mark from school? His family have just adopted a tiny puppy from the RSPCA. He might be there. He's called –'

Cassie came to an abrupt stop. Sarah heard a garbled *aaarghh* and turned around to see her friend flat on the floor with a large black-and-white dog on top of her! Sarah didn't know what to do. But then she realised that Cassie was laughing so hard that she could hardly breathe. Sarah exhaled with relief. Clearly this dog was friend, not foe.

Cassie managed to get herself into a sitting position but was still full of giggles.

'Calm down, Florence! Yes, it's great to see you too. Now sit!'

The dog sat obediently and Cassie managed to get to her feet, straightening her hair, her school-bag and her slobbered-on face all in one smooth movement.

'So this is a friend of yours?' asked Sarah.

'Sarah, meet Florence and –' Cassie glanced back in the direction Florence had come from '– you know Ben Stoppard from school.'

A very embarrassed-looking Ben ran up to them.

'Hi, Ben. Lost something?' asked Cassie.

'No!' He spluttered, staring furtively back the way he'd come. 'No, it's just that Florence got away from me. You know what she's like.'

He was breathless from running across the park. 'She must have seen you. She just took off! Are you okay?' Ben regained his breath and flicked his floppy hair back as he picked up the end of his dog's lead. Florence smiled beautifully at each of them and continued to sit.

'I'm fine!' said Cassie. 'No harm done, though some doggy breath-freshener wouldn't go amiss. Eau de Dog Breath is definitely *not* my favourite fragrance.'

'What are you two up to?' asked Ben as he looked back into the park again.

'We're just heading home for a milk-shake,' said Cassie. 'Sarah's staying with me for three days and we have some serious planning to do for tonight!'

'That sounds great!' said Ben. 'What's the flavour of the day?'

Both Cassie and Sarah stopped and stared at him.

'Let me rephrase that for you,' said Cassie. '*Sarah and I* are going home to plan *our super-girly sleepover* over a milkshake. Just so there's no confusion, that is, *a sleepover for girls*, talking about *girl's stuff*. Maybe we'll see you later back here? I promised Mrs Stephens that I'll take Rusty out for a walk.'

Ben was still looking uneasily over his

shoulder and seemed keen to leave the park quickly.

'I'll just join you for the milkshake bit, then. Come on, let's go.'

Ben was behaving very strangely and the girls weren't sure his ears were working properly either. He was definitely up to something.

Cassie and Sarah glanced back into the park to see what he might be avoiding, but could see nothing except a gaggle of small children and lots of dogs.

'Okay,' they agreed. 'But only for the milkshake bit!'

Chapter Two

'Here we go! Three choc-anilla-berry milkshakes!'

Cassie's mum, Samantha, put the tray of frothy-topped loveliness on the table outside the deli and took a seat herself. 'Nice to see you and Florence paying us a visit, Ben,' she said with a warm smile.

Ben and his family had moved from interstate a few months earlier, and he'd been a bit stand-offish with the Bannermans, especially Cassie, to begin with. But their love of animals brought them together and now they were firm friends.

'Delicious milkshake – thanks, Sam,' said Ben happily. Sounds of loud slurping filled the air. Gladiator was purring contentedly on Cassie's lap. Florence and Ripper lay stretched out under the table, enjoying each other's company.

'I'm going to be busy here this afternoon, Cass, at least until your dad gets back,' said Sam.

'That's okay, Mum. We're going to head back to the park for a while. Mrs Stephens' ankle is still not great, so I said I'd take Rusty out for a bit of a run with Ripper.'

10

'Right, well I'd better get back to work,' said Sam. 'I know Dad's made his super-special lasagne for dinner tonight, in honour of our special guest; so don't arrive late. You won't forget Ruby, will you, Sarah?'

'I won't. We'll pop in on the way to the park and have a little play. I have the house key here in my pocket! And we'll be back in plenty of time for dinner. I love lasagne!' Sarah slurped up the last of her milkshake and Ben and Cassie followed suit. They were ready for action!

'Sarah only lives in the next street,' Cassie explained to Ben as they leashed up the dogs.

'And I'm in charge of my cat Ruby while Mum and Dad are away,' said Sarah proudly.

'She'll love the company after being on her own all day and she likes dogs! Well, most dogs anyway.' Sarah looked a little worriedly at Florence. She really was rather large. Florence's gentle smile set her mind at ease and off they all went.

Sarah used her key and pushed the door open. Everything was the same as it had been this morning, but the house felt different with no-one else at home. Sarah was glad that she had her friends with her. She was feeling a bit spooked. In her own house! Too weird.

'Hey, Ruby! I'm home, puss. Come on,

bubba, it's dinner time!' she called out as they went in. 'That's funny. She usually comes running as soon as anyone opens the door. She loves company! Ru-by!'

'I bet she'll be all curled up asleep somewhere, enjoying the peace and quiet,' said Cassie. 'But don't worry, Ripper will find her!'

Ripper adopted his 'down to business' pose and started sniffing round the kitchen. In the living room, Florence attempted a 'down to business' pose too, but failed quite miserably and in her comical attempt, knocked over a large vase of flowers that had been sitting on the coffee table.

'Oops, sorry about that,' said Ben, grabbing the vase before it landed on the floor.

'Uh, Ben, maybe you and Florence might be better off checking out the garden?' Sarah suggested tactfully while grabbing a cloth and mopping up the spilled water. 'She's really an indoor cat, but there is a cat flap so she can go out if she wants to.'

'Or maybe,' added Cassie, slightly less tactfully, 'it might be time for you to go, Ben? Unless, of course, you wanted to join us for our sleepover? We could paint your toenails any colour you like! There'll be singing and dancing, cupcake baking . . .'

Ben was already heading for the front door with a grin. 'Okay, point taken, Cass. Come on, Florence, we know when we're not appreciated. See you later then.'

The door slammed shut after Ben and Florence. The girls grinned.

Sarah popped the flowers back in the vase. 'Good as new!' she said to herself as she dusted the orange pollen off her hands.

Suddenly they heard a single sharp bark coming in the direction of the kitchen. Cassie and Sarah ran towards the sound.

Chapter Three

In the kitchen, Cassie and Sarah saw Ripper sitting there calmly beside Ruby's food bowl.

'Oh, I thought he must have found her!' said Sarah, who was starting to worry. 'Never mind, let's keep looking.'

But as they turned to go, Ripper gave the same sharp bark. They both jumped.

'What's Ripper trying to tell us? Ruby's hardly touched the food I left out for her this morning,' said Sarah. 'It's odd that she'd leave that much behind. She's usually a good eater.'

'Yes, but look at this!' said Cassie.

Ripper relaxed and gently rolled his eyes. At last, he seemed to say, must I spell it out?

'There is nothing that looks more like cat-sick than, well, cat-sick,' said Cassie. 'Good boy, Ripper! If she has an upset tummy, chances are she's hiding out somewhere feeling sorry for herself.'

'But what if she's been sick all day and we never knew? Poor Ruby. Where are you, puss, puss?' Sarah was feeling anxious as she and Cassie renewed their search. They

18

flew through the house checking out all of Ruby's favourite spots. There were a lot of them. Linen cupboard, toy box, bathroom sink, vegetable crate, snuggled against Dad's pillow, top of the bookcase, sunny spot halfway into Jack's closet . . .

Ruby seemed to have disappeared into thin air.

Then there was another bark, this time from the garden, and Cassie went running out the back door. Ripper was sitting beside a bush. Ruby, barely visible, was lying motionless beside him.

'She's here, Sarah!' yelled Cassie. 'Ripper found her.'

'Phew,' whispered Sarah as she ran down the stairs and into the garden.

Cassie wore a grim expression. 'She

doesn't look well,' said Cassie, stroking Ruby as Sarah reached her.

'What do you mean? Do you think she's still sick?' said Sarah, alarmed.

Ruby was very still and although her eyes were open and blinking every now and again, she didn't seem to be focusing on anything. She didn't even turn towards Sarah as she patted her gently.

'I think there's definitely something wrong,' said Cassie as the girls gently manoeuvred Ruby out from under the bush.

Ripper, sensing the seriousness of the situation, kept watch on everything from a respectful distance.

Sarah was fighting back tears as she and Cassie felt all over Ruby's body for any sign of injury. There was nothing. No blood or cuts that would indicate she may have been in a fight. She didn't appear to have broken any bones and didn't really even seem to be in any pain.

'Oh, Ruby! I'm so sorry!' sobbed Sarah, giving in to her tears. 'Mum left me in charge, and now look! Poor puss!'

Cassie did her best to calm her friend, gently picked up the cat and placed her across Sarah's lap. Cassie was sure that it would make both of them feel better.

She ran back into the house and grabbed a cat box and fleecy blanket from the laundry and returned to Sarah as quickly as she could.

'Let's put her carefully in this and we'll get her straight to the vet. It's not far and Ben's dad will be there; he'll know exactly what to do.'

Chapter Four

Within a few minutes they'd arrived at the Abbotts Hill RSPCA clinic. The waiting room was busy but Margaret, the receptionist, took one look at the two girls' worried expressions and came over to them. She knew Cassie from her frequent visits and offers to help with everything.

'Cassie, what's happened? Who do we have here?' she asked.

'Hi, Margaret, this is Ruby. She's Sarah's cat. We've just found her like this in the garden. She looks really sick.'

At that moment Ben's dad, Dr Joe Stoppard, stepped out of the treatment room.

'Hello, Cassie. Oh, who's this?' asked the vet, casting an appraising eye over Ruby in her cat box. 'You'd better bring her straight through. Margaret, could you keep an eye on Ripper for a few minutes?' he asked, ushering Cassie, Sarah and Ruby through to the treatment room.

Sarah gave Dr Joe a quick rundown of the situation as he gently lifted Ruby out of the cat box. His hands moved quickly over the cat, but his voice remained slow and steady.

'So you hadn't seen Ruby since this morning, Sarah? What time was that?'

'I fed her as normal at about seven o'clock and then Mum and Dad dropped me at Cassie's just a bit after that.'

'But she looked and acted the same as usual? There was nothing different about her?'

'No, she was fine. But we noticed she had thrown up during the day and she doesn't seem to have eaten much,' said Sarah.

'She's not on any medication from the vet?' asked Dr Joe.

'No,' answered Sarah. 'She's never ill!'

All the time Dr Joe was examining the sick cat. He opened her mouth and looked under her tongue and down her throat; he opened her eyes and looked closely at each one with his flashlight. He checked her pulse and her temperature and gently ran his hands over every bit of her. Ruby was so floppy and soft and uncomplaining that it was hard to believe that she was a real cat at all.

'Well, there are no broken bones, but her stomach is pretty tender. I think the first thing we need to do is to get some fluid back into her body. There's a risk that she could become badly dehydrated and we don't want that to happen. We'll put her on a drip. That will regulate the amount of fluid going into her body.'

The girls nodded, listening carefully.

'I'm also going to take a sample of her blood and urine so that we can test it to see what the problem is here. The results will take a while to come back from the lab, Sarah. So we won't really know what the problem is until then. But I'm thinking that, so far, everything is pointing to the possibility that Ruby has somehow swallowed poison.'

Sarah gulped.

'But how could she be poisoned, Dr Joe?' said Cassie. 'Who would do such a thing?'

Dr Joe started fixing up a drip and administering medicine.

'I'm sure nobody has done it on purpose, Cassie. There are so many things that are toxic to cats and dogs, which are completely harmless to humans. Has Ruby had access to garden chemicals or anything like that?'

'Mum keeps all that stuff locked away in the cupboard,' said Sarah. 'I have two little brothers and they get into everything, so Mum has child locks everywhere!'

Dr Joe gently opened Ruby's mouth and deposited a tablet at the back of her throat. 'These tablets I'm giving her are charcoal. They'll soak up any poison that's left in her tummy. The only other thing we can do is keep her hydrated and wait. If we knew exactly what she'd eaten, we might be able to do more. But we won't know that until the blood and urine tests comes back.'

'Will she be all right?' asked Sarah quietly.

Dr Joe put a reassuring hand on Sarah's shoulder. 'We'll do all we can, but I'm afraid

28

there are no guarantees. I'll stay in touch and let you know how we go.'

Cassie grasped Sarah's hand firmly, upset for her friend.

Chapter Five

'Ugh, that was awful!' said Sarah as they stepped out onto the street a few minutes later. 'She looked so ill! She's never stayed overnight at the vet before. It must be really bad.'

'You can't think like that, Sarah. Dr Joe is an awesome vet and if anyone can make Ruby well again, he can!'

They wandered back to the deli next door and brought Cassie's mum up to date with the events of the afternoon.

Sarah had felt brave in the clinic, but she could feel it wearing off now. She found herself wishing that her mum and dad were here so that she didn't have to feel so responsible.

'I just can't believe she was poisoned!' muttered Cassie. 'What could've happened? It's not as though Ruby is out and about all the time like some cats are. You've said Ruby's always at home.'

Sarah nodded her agreement.

'It's not as though your parents are in the habit of keeping bottles of poison all over the house, are they?' asked Cassie.

In spite of the solemn mood, Sarah found herself smiling at the idea. 'Nope.'

'Oh no!' exclaimed Cassie as she jumped out of her chair. 'I've forgotten all about Rusty. I promised Mrs Stephens I'd walk him today!'

'I'm sure she'll understand, Cassie,' said her mum. 'Just give her a call and let her know you could do it tomorrow instead.'

'I could I suppose, but poor Rusty will have been inside all day. He'll be driving Mrs Stephens nuts by now.' Cassie felt awful letting her down but felt too that she should really be looking after Sarah.

'I'll come with you,' said Sarah. 'I think I'll feel better outside. It might stop me from worrying about Ruby.'

Ripper gave a good long wriggly shake, and declared himself ready for a walk. He quite liked Rusty, even though he pretended not to. Blue heelers could be a bit bossy sometimes, but he knew deep down Rusty was one of the good guys.

Mrs Stephens was sorry to hear the news about Ruby and started telling them about a neighbour she'd once had who'd almost lost two cats to poisoning.

Sarah was trying hard not to listen, sure that it hadn't ended well, but Cassie was intrigued.

'So did she discover what had poisoned them?'

'Well, that's the funny thing!' declared Mrs Stephens. 'It turned out that she had poisoned them herself! By accident, of course. She loved salt. Whenever she made her lovely meat sauces she would pile on the salt, then give those sauces to the cats and they'd gobble them right up.'

Mrs Stephens loved telling a story and once she started, it was hard to get her to stop!

'She knew the cats liked the meat. But then they started getting sick and lethargic and she had to take them to the vet. The vet told her the cats shouldn't have so much salt in their diet. Simple as that. But, Cassie, those cats made a full recovery! And I bet Ruby will, too.'

Sarah gave a sigh of relief as Mrs

Stephens came to the end of her story and handed over Rusty's lead.

'Thanks so much for doing this, Cassie. Rusty and I both appreciate it. Another few days and my ankle will be right as rain again!' said Mrs Stephens as she shuffled back inside.

'See,' said Cassie to Sarah, 'those cats got better after being poisoned.' Cassie was determined to look on the bright side.

'Hmmm,' said Sarah, not completely convinced. 'But we only ever feed Ruby the best cat food or the same meat that Mum buys for us. She never gets leftovers, so it can't be salt.'

'It'd be good to know what it was though, wouldn't it?' suggested Cassie.

'Yes, it would,' agreed Sarah, perking up a bit. 'Dr Joe said he could do more to help her if he knew what she'd eaten!'

'Then let's find out!' declared Cassie.

Chapter Six

The girls were deep in conversation as they entered the park. So deep in fact that when they heard '*psssst*' they carried on walking. But when the '*psssst*' sounded a second time they stopped dead in their tracks.

'What was that?' said Sarah.

'*Psssst*, Cassie, Sarah!' They heard in a comical stage-whisper. 'It's me, Ben! Down here!'

Behind the lowest wall of the closest flowerbed, as far away from the dog-walking area of the park as it was possible to be, lay Ben. He was flat on his stomach with Florence lying quietly beside him.

'Is this some strange sort of obedience training?' said Sarah, turning towards Cassie for confirmation.

Cassie shook her head. She was as puzzled as Sarah.

'Cassie, is anyone looking over this way?' asked Ben.

'Uh, no. There's nobody here but me and Sarah,' said Cassie.

'You're sure?'

'Quite sure!' said Cassie. 'What are you doing down there?'

For the second time that day Ben seemed seriously embarrassed. He sat up slowly, still looking cautiously toward the dog area. Then he flicked his fringe back in an attempt to regain some small scrap of cool.

'Nothing. Just one of those things. I thought I dropped something . . .' Ben said, sounding very unconvincing.

'Okay then,' said Cassie, eyebrows raised.

'I think Florence and I have had enough running around for today. I might just carry on home,' said Ben.

Florence gave Rusty a jealous sniff on the way past. She didn't much like other dogs playing with her Ripper!

41

'Well, see you tomorrow then,' said Cassie. 'If your invisible stalker doesn't catch you first!' she added cheekily.

'So funny,' said Ben over his shoulder as he and Florence headed for the gate.

Cassie and Sarah looked at each other and began giggling.

While Ripper and Rusty rumbled and chased and ran and wrestled, Cassie and Sarah put their heads together. By the time the dogs were panting and ready for home, the girls had come up with a plan of action.

With a tired-out Rusty safely delivered back to Mrs Stephens, they retreated to the study in Cassie's house and turned on her mum's computer.

'Right!' said Cassie. 'Research!'

Sarah sat beside her with a notebook and pen, ready to list all the household things that might be toxic to cats.

There were a lot of them.

'But so many of these are things we encounter every day,' sighed Cassie.

'Like what?' said Sarah.

'Onion and garlic. They're both toxic to cats,' Cassie answered. The girls looked at each other, surprised.

'But we have those things sitting around in the kitchen all the time,' said Sarah.

'I guess they mean cooked onion that you might feed to your cat in leftovers,' said Cassie. 'Like Mrs Stephens' friend with the salt. But you said Ruby doesn't eat leftovers, so we can cross onions off the list.'

'Yes, but look,' said Sarah, pointing to the screen. 'What about chocolate? Tomatoes? Potatoes? Macadamias? Grapes? Avocado? Milk?'

Sarah carefully wrote them all down. 'I thought cats loved milk!'

'Lots of cats are lactose intolerant and milk upsets their stomach,' said Cassie, reading the information off the screen.

'Ruby never drinks milk, anyway. She prefers water,' remembered Sarah.

'This list goes on and on,' said Cassie, making a mental note of all the things she needed to check out round her own garden; chemicals, fertilisers, certain plants, detergents. It seemed endless.

Fifteen minutes later, equipped with Sarah's list and her house key, they set off back to Sarah's house.

Chapter Seven

'Okay then, Sarah,' said Cassie. 'Let's start over there at the bush where we found her. Is that her favourite place in the garden?'

'No, not at all,' said Sarah. 'She really prefers to be inside. Look at all the lovely things I've planted out here for her. Catnip and catmint – cats are supposed to love them. I thought they might tempt Ruby to come out more often to enjoy the sunshine and get some exercise, but they didn't really work. I guess she only likes the sunnier spots when it's not too hot.'

'There's no food left in the garden and the lid of the compost bin is shut, so she couldn't have gone rummaging round in there. Maybe the plants are more likely? Do you know the names of all these flowers, Sarah?'

'Not really. But you can look up the poisonous kinds on the internet. There'll be photos of each one. Here's the key. Mum's laptop is on the kitchen bench.'

'Good idea. And to save time, maybe you can check for any chemicals?'

suggested Cassie. 'Snail pellets, mouse or rat baits, fertilisers, anything like that. Your neighbour on that side has a pool,' she said, pointing. 'Ask them whether they might have left any chlorine lying around.'

Sarah nodded. 'That's a great plan of action, Cassie. I don't think Ruby ever leaves our garden, but I guess it wouldn't hurt to ask anyway. Let's get on with it!' she replied before running off.

Sarah quite enjoyed being busy for a while. It took her mind off Ruby and made her feel that she was doing something to help at the same time. When she asked her neighbour, he said he had never seen Ruby in his backyard. And in any case, they kept their pool chemicals under lock and key and didn't have trouble with rats, mice, slugs or snails, so there were no baits or pellets lying around.

Cassie was coming to the end of her search, too. The list of plants was a long one; azaleas, daffodils, lilies, irises . . . but none of the pictures she'd found online matched anything in Sarah's garden.

Even Ripper sensed the slump in mood and came to join the girls in the middle of the garden. They munched quietly on some biscuits Sarah found in the pantry before deciding that they'd really done all they could.

'It's getting late,' said Cassie, 'and I told

Mum we'd be in time for dinner. We should go. Come on.'

Cassie's dad had excelled himself in the kitchen and the lasagne was every bit as good as her mum had said it would be. But the mood at the table had been solemn.

'Would you like to ring your mum, Cassie?' said Sam as she cleared away the dishes. 'Let her know what's happened?'

'Do you think I should?' Sarah asked. She just couldn't decide what was the right thing to do. She really wanted to talk to her mum. She always made Sarah feel better and she'd realised that with all the excitement going on this afternoon, she'd forgotten her mum and dad wouldn't be there tonight to cheer her up with a hug and kiss before bed.

'But what if she wants to come home? They've waited a long time for this holiday and they were so looking forward to it. I don't want to spoil it for them!' Sarah confessed.

Sarah didn't think she could feel any worse than she already did, but the thought of telling her mum what had happened to Ruby was just too much. She even lost interest in her dessert. Lemon gelato!

'I think you should talk to her!' said Cassie, looking at the untouched gelato and making the decision for her.

Sam handed Sarah her mobile phone and gave her a big hug. 'Tell your mum that you've done everything you possibly could for Ruby, Sarah. I'll call her later for a chat too.'

Sarah went off to a quiet spot to talk to her mum. She felt happier already.

Chapter Eight

Later that evening, the girls were chatting quietly when they heard Samantha Bannerman shouting up the stairs.

'Cassie! Sarah! Dr Joe is here!'

They thundered down the stairs in their pyjamas without even considering the possibility that Ben might be there too.

He was.

'Oh! Hi, Ben,' squeaked Cassie, trying to hide behind the couch with Sarah rather than be seen in her pyjamas by a boy at eight o'clock in the evening.

To his credit, Ben only smirked ever so slightly. His dad, on the other hand, looked very serious. Cassie and Sarah glanced at each other and knew without being told that the news was not good.

'I don't have anything positive to report, girls.'

'Has she . . . died?' asked Sarah bravely.

'No, no, but she is unconscious.' Dr Joe looked over the heads of the girls at Cassie's parents and raised his eyebrows. Cassie turned around in time to see her mum's eyebrows go up too and then the slightest shrug; she knew even worse news was coming.

Ben's face was equally as grave as his father's.

'I'm sorry, Sarah, but there's a chance that she won't make it through the night,' continued Dr Joe. 'I'm afraid the results of the tests may just come too late. If we only knew what she'd eaten, there might be some hope.'

The girls quietly thanked Dr Joe and Ben for dropping in to let them know, even if the news was really bad.

Sam quietly showed the Stoppards to the door.

'Let's hope for the best, shall we?' said Cassie's dad as he came over and hugged both girls. 'Cats have nine lives. I bet Ruby has a few left, doesn't she?'

Sarah tried to smile. She really wanted to hope for the best but she couldn't, she just felt awful.

It was the quietest sleepover that Mr and Mrs Bannerman could ever remember.

Chapter Nine

It was morning, and before the girls were even dressed Ben was on the phone.

'Cassie! I think you and Sarah missed an important clue yesterday!' Ben announced excitedly. 'Something that Sarah said when we were at her house.'

'Well, tell me, Ben! It's too early for

twenty questions! What clue?' Cassie was not a morning person.

'She said that Ruby preferred to be inside the house. She's an indoor cat, but you said you spent the whole afternoon checking out the garden,' said Ben.

'So whatever poisoned Ruby might have come from inside the house!' concluded Cassie.

'Exactly. I'll meet you at Sarah's in ten minutes,' said Ben.

Despite her concern, Sarah had had a good night's sleep. She was optimistic about the search and she appreciated her friends'

efforts. If her cat could be saved, then Sarah would do what she could!

She and Cassie walked over to Sarah's house. As they reached the gate, they heard someone calling out, 'Cassie, Cassie!'

A little girl, already dressed for school, came running towards them, and both Cassie and Sarah recognised her as one of the tiniest kindergarteners at school.

'Hi, Amy!' said Cassie. 'You're up and about early. What's the matter?'

'I was just wondering if you've seen Ben this morning?'

'Ben Stoppard? No, but we're just on our way to meet him now. How do you know Ben?' Cassie was surprised.

'He's my reading buddy!' said Amy. 'I'm turning five tomorrow and I'm having a

party and I've been looking for Ben all week to give him this!' She held up a gorgeous handmade glittery party invitation. 'Do you think he might want to come?' she asked, staring up at them with big brown eyes.

'I'm sure he'd love to! Just leave it up to me!' said Cassie as she slipped the invitation into her pocket.

'Thanks, Cassie!' Amy chirped before skipping off, as happy as could be.

'Aha!' said Cassie in triumph, turning to Sarah. 'I think we have just discovered Ben's invisible stalker. She's real . . .'

'And tiny,' added Sarah.

'And totally unscary!' finished up Cassie.

Cassie and Sarah were still chuckling as they opened the door of Sarah's house.

Before they'd even had time to shut the door behind them, Ben appeared.

'Morning, Ben! Any invisible stalkers this morning? I thought I saw one lurking outside wearing our school uniform?' asked Cassie.

Ben looked very uneasy for a moment. They couldn't possibly know, could they? No, he was fairly sure Cassie was bluffing.

'Let's check the bathrooms first and the kitchen,' said Ben, quickly changing the subject.

They split up and spread out over the house but soon came back disheartened. The house was clean and tidy. The bins and toilets had their lids firmly down. The cleaning cupboards were well locked.

'This house is like a cat paradise!' declared Cassie as she stepped over a huge scratching post on her way into the living room. 'No wonder Ruby prefers to be inside. There are comfortable little cat nooks all over the place. I bet she loves this one!' she said, pointing to a small basket hanging under the coffee table. It was catching the morning sun and looked super-cosy.

'It's her favourite,' Sarah admitted. 'I think she likes this room best because it's quiet.'

'It smells nice, too!' said Ben.

'Actually, it does smell good. I hadn't noticed!' said Sarah. 'That'll be Mum's anniversary flowers. Dad always gets –'

The light-bulb moment hit all three children at the same instant.

A huge vase full of beautiful white waxy lilies. The flowers were gorgeous . . . and toxic to cats! They were one of the flowers Cassie had noticed when she was researching plants the day before. 'But why would she have eaten them?' said Sarah.

'She probably didn't. See that orangey dust? It's the pollen,' Cassie explained. 'It's almost as poisonous to cats as the rest of the plant. It's fallen onto the table and Ruby's water bowl is nearby. She probably didn't even taste it.'

Ben was already on his mobile phone, letting his dad know of their discovery.

'You know,' said Sarah, 'I don't think I'd make a very good detective. Florence knocked that whole vase over yesterday and I picked up the flowers without even thinking. The pollen was really hard to wash off! I had a bright orange clue on my hands all evening and didn't even realise!'

Chapter Ten

Nine o'clock was fast approaching and Ben, Cassie and Sarah were hurrying to get to school before the bell rang.

They'd had a busy morning already. They'd raced to the clinic to find that Ruby had survived the night. Even better, she'd regained consciousness. She still looked very ill and would need to stay on the drip for another few days.

'I can't tell you how lucky she is, Sarah,' said Dr Joe. 'Every part of the lily is poisonous to cats, and if she'd eaten more she would almost certainly have died. She must have swallowed the tiniest bit of pollen to be on the mend already. Great detective work from all of you. Can I suggest you tell your dad to buy roses for your mum next time?'

Sarah was overjoyed when Ruby seemed to recognise her. She even purred gently when Sarah stroked her tummy.

'It is going to be okay!' Sarah decided. 'I can't believe she's better!' Cassie's mum had promised to ring Sarah's mum and let her know about the improvement in Ruby's health.

'Oh, Ben,' said Cassie, digging deep into her pocket as they reached the school gates. 'Before I forget! Sweet little Amy Barker asked me to give you this.' She handed the party invitation to Ben with a big smile. 'It's on tomorrow after school and Amy was really worried that she might not see you before then, so I said I'd make sure it got to you. Should be great!'

Ben held the invitation as though it smelled really bad and his face turned the same colour as the paper. Really quite bright pink.

'How do you know Amy?' Ben was surprised.

Sarah interrupted. 'Cassie knows everyone in Abbotts Hill, Ben.'

Cassie nodded. 'It's true.'

'But she's been following me round for a week!' said Ben, finally letting his exasperation out. 'Ever since we did the Buddy Reading that day. She's driving me crazy! Everywhere I go, she's there! It's so embarrassing! She watches me play soccer, she comes running over to me every time I set foot in the dog park with Florence. My friends think it's hilarious, but there is no way I am going to a party with hundreds of five-year-old girls!' Ben sounded desperate.

Cassie and Sarah were doubled over in hysterics by the time Ben finished his rant.

'You may be happy to know Amy has a bit of a reputation for finding new friends . . . and sticking to them like glue,' said Sarah, wiping tears of laughter from her eyes. 'Amy was besotted with my brother Jack last term. But it was only a week before she found someone new to befriend.'

Cassie giggled. 'That's right. There was Tom Burrow from year four a few weeks ago. He had to turn down an invitation from Amy to go to the zoo.'

Sarah grinned. 'I remember now. He pretended he had chicken pox for the weekend.'

Ben looked abashed. 'Oh, I didn't realise,' he said. 'She is really sweet. And I feel better about the whole thing now that I know it's not just me.'

'Well, if you'd just asked us rather than running around looking like you were hiding from the secret police . . .' said Cassie cheekily.

The bell rang.

'Better go,' said Ben, running off to class, school bag and legs flying in all directions.

'Thanks for your help with saving Ruby,' called out Sarah to his retreating back.

'Any time,' he said, before almost careering into the vice-principal.

Cassie looked after him, thoughtful. 'The more I think about it, the more I realise Ben Stoppard behaves an awful lot like his dog.'

Sarah laughed. 'I've always thought that you and Ripper are like each other too.'

Cassie was about to get offended, and then she stopped. 'I guess you're right. We are quite similar.'

The girls hurried off to class, giggling.

'Tonight our proper sleepover begins, okay?' said Sarah.

'Pizza, gelato and a movie?' suggested Cassie.

'Count me in!' answered Sarah.

RSPCA

ABOUT THE RSPCA

The RSPCA is the country's best known and most respected animal welfare organisation. The first RSPCA in Australia was formed in Victoria in 1871, and the organisation is now represented by RSPCAs in every state and territory.

The RSPCA's mission is to prevent cruelty to animals by actively promoting their care and protection. It is a not-for-profit charity that is firmly based in the Australian community, relying upon the support of individuals, businesses and organisations to survive and continue its vital work.

Every year, RSPCA shelters throughout Australia accept over 150,000 sick, injured or abandoned animals from the community.

The RSPCA believes that every animal is entitled to the Five Freedoms:

Fact File

- freedom from hunger and thirst (ready access to fresh water and a healthy, balanced diet)
- freedom from discomfort, including accommodation in an appropriate environment that has shelter and a comfortable resting area
- freedom from pain, injury or disease through prevention or rapid diagnosis and providing veterinary treatment when required

- freedom to express normal behaviour, including sufficient space, proper facilities and company of the animal's own kind and
- freedom from fear and distress through conditions and treatment that avoid suffering.

HOW TO KEEP YOUR HOUSEHOLD PET SAFE FROM POISON

Many common household items such as food, plants and medicines are fatally toxic to our pets. It is important to be aware of the most commonly found poisons so that they are not kept within reach of your pet.

Rodent poisons and insecticides

These are one of the most common causes of pet poisonings. Poisons such as rat and snail bait should be used with extreme caution. If you must use rodenticides or insecticides, keep them safely locked up and only use them in areas of your property that are inaccessible to your dog or cat.

Medication

Many prescription and over-the-counter medications are toxic to animals. Paracetamol is a commonly found pain medication that is

Fact File

particularly poisonous to cats, even in tiny amounts. Never medicate your pet without the advice of your veterinarian and make sure that all medications are kept in sealed containers, out of the reach of your pets. Some pet medicines can also be dangerous to your pet if used incorrectly. For example, some flea-prevention treatments for dogs contain compounds that are highly toxic to cats.

Food

Some foods are toxic to your pets and should never be given to them. These include chocolate, onions and garlic (including products containing onion or garlic powder, e.g. baby food), tomatoes (for cats), macadamia nuts, raisins, grapes and products containing caffeine.

Feeding fat trimmings may cause your pet to develop pancreatitis, and foods such as raw fish, liver and sugary foods can lead to metabolic diseases when fed in excess.

Fact File

Avocado is toxic to many animals, including birds, dogs, mice, rabbits, horses and livestock.

Be careful not to feed your pets cooked bones, as these can splinter and can cause gastrointestinal obstructions and injury.

Common plants and mulch
Some common house and garden plants are deadly to animals if ingested. These include Lily species, Brunfelsia species (Yesterday-today-and-tomorrow) and cycad seeds. Cocoa mulch is also highly toxic if ingested.

Fact File

Fertilizers

RSPCA Australia recommends that owners take active steps to ensure that their dogs and other pets do not ingest any type of fertilizer material. If an owner suspects their dog or other pet has ingested fertilizer, they should contact their local vet immediately for further advice.

Fertilizer products generally contain varying amounts of nitrogen (N), phosphorus (P) and potassium (K) compounds. They may have additives such as herbicides, insecticides, fungicides, iron, copper and zinc. Because fertilizers are usually a combination of ingredients, the effects following ingestion may differ.

In general, fertilizers cause mild to moderate gastrointestinal irritation that may involve signs such as vomiting, diarrhoea, hypersalivation, lethargy and abdominal pain. In most cases the effects are self-limiting and can be resolved within 24-48 hours with supportive veterinary care.

Lost in Translation

Helen Kelly

RANDOM HOUSE AUSTRALIA

Chapter One

Cassie Bannerman flipped over the sign on the deli window from 'closed' to 'open' and unlocked the door. Her dad, Alex, was already getting the coffee machine ready for the morning rush and she took a seat at the counter to finish her breakfast. The gorgeous cheese and bacon muffin was still warm from the oven. Her dad had been up for hours, getting the day's baking done before she had even left for school. She was about to tell him for the millionth time that he really was the best baker in the world, when the door jangled open and Dr Joe Stoppard, the vet from the RSPCA clinic and shelter further up the street, wandered in looking very much in need of coffee.

'Morning, Dr Joe!' said Cassie. Dr Joe was often the first customer of the day and usually stayed for a bit of a chat. Cassie loved animals and one day hoped to become a vet herself, so she was always interested to hear about the comings and goings at the RSPCA.

'Ah, perfect! Just the thing,' said Dr Joe as Alex put down a beautifully brewed cup of coffee on the counter in front of him.

Gladiator, Cassie's beloved tabby cat, swaggered over and gently leapt onto Cassie's lap. After a bit of a wriggle to find the comfiest spot, he purred himself loudly to sleep.

'Gladiator came from our RSPCA shelter, didn't he, Cassie?' asked Dr Joe.

'Yes he did, but way before you first arrived here. He was a tiny kitten then and now he's just about as big as he could be. He must be four years old,' said Cassie, stroking the sleeping cat.

'Well, we're hoping there are lots of other people like you out there who will give a kitten a loving home in the next few weeks,' said Dr Joe as he took his first sip of coffee.

'Yesterday an inspector brought in

a mother cat that had been found on some unused bushland near the tennis courts. She was doing her best to feed a litter of six kittens. They're tiny, even though I think they're about eight weeks old. Both mum and kittens are badly malnourished, but I think a few good meals and lots of TLC will see them come good.'

'Six kittens!' squeaked Cassie.

'Make that eleven kittens . . .' said Dr Joe.

'Eleven?' Cassie was confused.

'Yes. We were just closing up last night when an elderly lady came in with a big box. A mother cat had given birth to five kittens in her garden shed! The mother is microchipped, but we haven't been able to locate her owner yet. The babies are only a few days old; their eyes aren't even open.

They're lucky to be alive, really. It's been pretty cold at night.'

'Goodness, the cattery at the shelter must be overflowing,' mused Cassie.

'Yes, the new holding area was finished just in the nick of time,' said Dr Joe. 'Though it still looks a bit basic. We might need to raise some funds before we can get it properly equipped, but in the meantime it's good to have the extra space.'

'Ha! Wait until they all start growing and running around,' said Cassie. 'It'll be a complete madhouse!'

'They'll be with us for a while too,' added Dr Joe. 'They need to be around twelve weeks old before we can adopt them out, and then only if they're in perfect health,' said Dr Joe.

'Hey, Dr Joe, you could turn part of the new holding area into a kitten playground,' suggested Cassie.

'There'd certainly be plenty of space now and it'd be great that they could be out in the fresh air, all together and yet still safely closed in,' agreed Dr Joe.

'You'd need a lot of new stuff, though,' Cassie pondered aloud. 'Scratching posts and some of those towers, so the kittens could jump from one to the other. And lots of balls and bells and tunnels, of course!'

Alex looked over at Joe and they both shook their heads slightly while they tried not to smile. When Cassie was on a roll, there was really no stopping her.

'And litter! You're going to be needing so much more litter,' she continued.

Dr Joe was finishing up his coffee and was about to leave when Cassie's chatter came to a sudden stop and she jumped to her feet. The forgotten Gladiator was not impressed and grouchily glared at Cassie before sloping off to find a more relaxing place to snooze.

'Dr Joe, you need to raise funds for the kittens right now. I'm going to think of something that will raise enough money to create a playground for them!' Cassie was very excited.

'Now that,' said Dr Joe, 'is a great idea!'

'I just have to think of the perfect thing to do,' Cassie went on. 'Maybe a sponsored walk? Or a raffle? What about a cake sale? Guess the weight of the kitten?'

'Why don't you pop in this afternoon?'

said Dr Joe. He was well aware that it might be some time before Cassie ran out of ideas and he didn't want to be late for work. 'Ben is coming over to have a look at the kittens. Perhaps you can get him interested in your fundraising idea. I'm sure the two of you will come up with something.'

'Sounds perfect. Thanks, Dr Joe. I'd love to see the kittens!' said Cassie.

'Thanks for the coffee, Alex. I'm ready to face the day,' said Dr Joe, getting up and walking towards the door. 'It's going to be a busy one. Not only is the shelter overrun with cats, but within a few minutes it's going to be overrun with students too!'

'Vet students?' asked Alex.

'Yes, four of them. They're all in their first year of university studying Vet Science.

I think I'll have my work cut out for me today!' said Dr Joe as he headed out into the sunshine.

'Bye, Dr Joe,' Cassie yelled after him, her mind still racing with ideas for the fundraiser.

Chapter Two

'So how much are you hoping to raise?' asked Ben.

'Well, I don't know, as much as we can. Anything at all will help. We just need to think of something that will attract people's attention and make them want to give us their money,' said Cassie as the two friends walked home from school. 'My head's been bursting with ideas all day,' she said, 'and I've eventually narrowed it down to my Top Ten Fundraising Ideas!'

With that, Cassie drew a huge piece of paper from her schoolbag and handed it to Ben. It was filled with writing from top to bottom.

'That's way more than ten!' said Ben, appalled that she might actually make him read them all.

'Okay, maybe fifteen. Twenty, tops, but they're all good ideas! I thought we could read through them together and decide which one would be best,' said Cassie.

Ben glanced down the list while Cassie continued to chatter away.

'If we did it at the dog park on a busy

Saturday, there would be a lot of people with pets around. We could make some big, colourful posters and put them up all over the place before then so that everyone would know about it in advance and bring money.'

In spite of himself, Ben was being dragged in. Cassie's enthusiasm was infectious, and as he glanced down Cassie's list of admittedly great ideas, Ben had one of his own.

'So, which one do you like best?' she asked.

'It's not one that's on the list, but I think it could be good. Better than good; it could be huge!' said Ben.

'What is it?' Cassie demanded.

'How about a charity dog-wash?' He

paused uncertainly, and when Cassie didn't say anything he ploughed on. 'We could do it at the dog park and charge ten dollars for each dog. It'd be great fun too, don't you think?' Ben thought it really was a fabulous idea but he'd rarely seen Cassie speechless. Was she annoyed that he hadn't picked one from her list?

Finally she spoke. 'Ben!' she shrieked. 'That is brilliant! It's a perfect idea. Wow, that's fantastic!'

'Okay, Cassie, calm down. You're scaring me now.' Ben grinned. 'We could set up by the gate where there are two water taps,' he continued. 'Have a hose each going in separate directions. We'd need lots of doggy shampoo, but that's all. We wouldn't have to buy anything else.'

'Mum's still got my old baby bathtub in the garage. We could get someone else to join in too and wash the small dogs in the bath,' added Cassie.

'Yeah! Hey I bet we could wash a hundred dogs if we were there all day!'

'Why don't we do it this Saturday?' suggested Ben.

'Sure. That gives us days and days to get everything ready. I could do a poster tonight. Your dad is going to love this!' said Cassie as they reached the clinic and went inside.

Chapter Three

Once inside, Cassie and Ben were surprised to be greeted by a young man in a clean white doctor's coat.

'And what can we do for you today?' he asked. 'Do you have an appointment? Or for that matter, do you have a pet?' he added, looking around them as if to see whether there might be a chance that they were concealing a large dog.

'Oh, um...' Ben and Cassie looked at each other as though they might have walked into the wrong place. 'Is Margaret around?' asked Ben.

'I'm over here, Ben! Hi Cassie!' Margaret shouted over from the reception desk. 'This is Peter, one of our work-experience students. It's okay, Peter, this is Dr Joe's son, Ben, and his friend Cassie.'

From behind the stacks and stacks of files piled up on the reception desk popped up one, and then two heads. Within seconds two more students wearing pristine white coats appeared from behind the counter.

'Hello, Ben and Cassie, I'm Grace,'

said a smart-looking girl with beautiful long dark hair.

'I'm Michael,' said a tanned boy with an athletic build. 'It's very nice to meet you both.'

Ben and Cassie didn't know what to say. The vet students were so confident and . . . tall!

'Ah, have you enjoyed your first day?' Cassie managed to ask before the door opened behind them and the fourth white-coated student appeared.

'Oh, another one,' said Cassie with an uncertain smile.

Now Cassie and Ben were completely surrounded by the students.

'Hello,' said the newcomer, and she hurried past them.

'And that's Lauren,' said Peter.

Lauren glanced back with a little smile and then carried on towards Margaret.

'Did you get to watch Dad in action?' asked Ben.

'Yes!' Grace, Michael and Peter said all together.

'It was fascinating! We watched two different dogs undergo surgery,' started Grace.

'Yes, one had been knocked down by a car and had broken his leg badly, but your dad was great!' continued Michael.

'He'll be right as rain in a few weeks!' said Peter.

'And the other had swallowed a piece of Lego,' said Grace.

'And your dad had to put the little

camera down his throat to see just how far it had gone before deciding the best way to remove it.'

'He's fantastic!'

'And the cat. Don't forget the cat.'

'He needed six stitches across his head after getting into a fight with a wire fence.'

'Poor thing.'

'And now we're having a look at some of your dad's old cases.'

Cassie and Ben were losing track of who was saying what. The students were so enthusiastic and all spoke at once. Just then the consulting room door opened and his dad came towards them.

The three students moved as a unit; they just seemed to gravitate towards Dr Joe, and the children were forgotten.

'Did you need us, Dr Joe? Is there something you'd like us to do?' they all asked.

Dr Joe was looking a bit frazzled and Ben understood why. These students were really something else!

Chapter Four

'I think a bit of fresh air is in order,' declared Dr Joe a little desperately.

He had four dog leashes in one hand and four dog singlets in the other. Each singlet was bright blue and had the words 'I'm looking for a home. Interested in adopting a dog? Speak to my walker!' emblazoned across the back.

'Take one of these each,' he said, handing them out. 'Where's Lauren?' he asked, looking around.

'I'm here, Dr Joe. Sorry I was just finishing off –' she began as she came towards them.

'It's okay,' said Dr Joe, cutting her off. 'Just follow me.' He turned on his heel and strode towards the dog-holding area, the students fluttering along behind him.

Cassie and Ben looked at each other and shrugged before following them out.

'This is Bill,' said Dr Joe, introducing a large, cheery-looking, middle-aged man. 'Bill's one of our favourite volunteers and one of our most experienced dog walkers. He's been coming in two evenings a week for over ten years and there is nothing that he doesn't know about dogs! Today, you're all going to help him,' said Dr Joe to the students. 'You met all the dogs earlier, and now Bill has selected a dog for each of you to take for a walk.

'He'll show you where our local park is. There's a fantastic leash-free area in the middle that's fenced in and huge. It's perfect for a really good run. The dogs will wear the singlets, and you'll find that a fair few people will stop to chat about the adoption program and ask for info. Okay, everyone?'

The students were ready for action. As though Dr Joe had fired a starting pistol, they flew towards the dogs like a busy swarm of bees.

Within minutes the dogs and students were lined up and ready to go. Bill was like a Sergeant Major. They walked out two by two. Peter and Bill led the pack with twin German shepherds called Morris and Maud firmly at heel. Then came Michael and Grace; Michael with Muddle, an energetic young kelpie, and Grace with a whippet called Bones, who was almost as elegant as herself. Lauren trailed behind the others with a timid, doe-eyed little bitser called Colin.

'I'll keep them out for an hour; they'll come back exhausted,' said Bill with a wink, leaving Dr Joe to wonder whether he meant the dogs or the students.

Dr Joe turned to Cassie and Ben with a sigh of relief.

'Oh yes, the kittens!' he said. And he turned on his heel once more.

DOG

The cattery was quiet and subdued compared to the rest of the shelter and Dr Joe seemed altogether calmer and more subdued himself.

He pointed to a large cage that had a sack covering the front of it to create a nice dark space inside.

'The kittens are in here,' he said and pulled the cloth cover open halfway. Cassie and Ben peered in and saw five tiny kittens all huddled together beside mum, fast asleep.

'Any luck with the microchip, Dr Joe?' whispered Cassie.

'No, nothing yet,' he replied. 'There's no response from the phone number that's on record. But it's early days. I'm sure someone is missing her; she's been well taken care of. What we do know is that her name is Peppermint.'

'Aww, that's so sweet,' cooed Cassie.

Ben laughed. 'Yeah, good one, Cassie, sweet! Peppermint? Sweet? Get it?'

'So lame,' said Cassie and tried to ignore him.

'Apart from keeping mum well fed, there's really not much we need to do for them right now,' said Dr Joe. 'Just provide a warm, comfortable and quiet environment until they're a bit bigger. They're all in good health, which is lucky,'

Cassie took one last look at the kittens before replacing the cloth and following Dr Joe and Ben into the next room.

'The second lot are in the exercise pen with mum. You can watch them play and then we'll round them up for bed,' said Dr Joe.

'I love your idea about the kitty playground, Cassie,' said Dr Joe, as they watched the tiny kittens crawling and tumbling over each other. 'They really would benefit from the fresh air and just being in a bigger space. Did you think any more about the fundraiser?'

'Of course! It's all decided and the date is set!' said Cassie.

Chapter Five

Later that same evening Cassie was sitting in her favourite homework spot, the table closest to the counter in the deli. The table was scattered with every colour of texta you could imagine and several large sheets of discarded paper.

'Okay, this is the one, Mum. What do

you think?' she said as she held her finished masterpiece up for inspection.

'Wow, it looks very professional! Those colours are really going to stand out. And you've got all the information you need,' said Sam as she read down the page.

Charity dog wash!
This Saturday at the Abbotts Hill Dog Park.
9am–4pm
$10 per dog.
Raising money to help kittens in need at the RSPCA.
See you there.
Don't forget your dog!

'That's great, Cass! It covers everything and your pictures are gorgeous. It's definitely an eye-catcher,' said Sam. 'I might send one to the fundraising people at the RSPCA. I called them today to let them know what you've got planned. They thought it was a great idea and wished you the best of luck.'

'Thanks, Mum. I can't wait until Saturday!' said Cassie.

At that moment, just as Sam was thinking she could probably shut up shop for the night, the deli door opened and a whole group of customers came chattering up to the counter and ordered coffees, hot chocolates and muffins before plonking themselves down at the table across from Cassie's.

Cassie started to clear away her things when she realised that the chattering had stopped and the entire group of new arrivals was looking her way!

'Cassie!' said one of them. 'We met you earlier at the clinic!'

'Oh, hello,' said Cassie, recognising Dr Joe's work-experience students. 'You look different without your white coats on. Have you just finished?'

'Yes,' said Grace, 'we've had such a great day. But what's this you're doing? School project?'

'No, it's just a fundraising thing that Ben and I are doing on Saturday. We're going to try to wash as many dogs as we can to raise money for Dr Joe to spend on the new kittens,' said Cassie as the students passed her poster around so they could all read it.

It was agreed loudly and enthusiastically that the whole idea was wonderful! By the time the students had all read to the bottom of the page, Cassie had enlisted three willing helpers for Saturday and the whole thing looked as though it was going to be as huge as Ben had predicted.

When the students discovered that Cassie wanted to be a vet when she grew up, they spent the next half hour passing on tips and funny stories about their learning experiences.

Cassie was a bit overwhelmed by all the attention. As she looked down the table she realised for the first time that Lauren was there too. The student was slowly sipping tea and seemed happy to let the conversation drift along without her. Cassie wondered if Lauren wasn't as overwhelmed by the other students as she was.

'Well, we better get going!' said Peter,

and the students all stood up. 'Another busy day at the surgery tomorrow, doctors,' he joked. The group left the deli, sounding like a noisy gaggle of geese.

'Switch that sign to closed, would you, Cass?' yelled Sam. 'Let's get this lot sorted out and we'll go and have some dinner,' she said as she came round the counter to clear the table.

She jumped as she saw Lauren and then laughed at herself. 'Oh, sorry, you gave me a bit of a surprise! I thought you'd all left together. Can I get you something else?'

'No, no, sorry,' said Lauren, who was the picture of embarrassment. 'I didn't realise you were closing. I'd better move.'

'Ha!' laughed Cassie. 'Do it carefully or you'll get the Death Stare.'

'Mmm . . .' said Lauren, smiling for the first time. 'I'm quite familiar with the Death Stare.'

Sam stared at them as though they'd both gone mad until she spotted Gladiator. Though the cat appeared very comfortable on Lauren's lap, he had one eye open looking around suspiciously. Sam laughed. 'He's big, but he wouldn't hurt a flea.' She grabbed Gladiator and headed towards his cat bowl. 'Dinnertime for the furry member of the household.'

Chapter Six

By the time Sam came back with three frothy mugs of hot chocolate, Cassie and Lauren were chatting away like old friends.

'It's so different to being at university,' Lauren was saying. 'Today was the first time I'd seen an actual operation. Of course we've all done the theory, but when it came to the real thing, Dr Joe was firing off questions like '*How would you restrain that cat?*' and '*What size needle would I use for this?*' and I just stood there all tongue-tied. I don't think I managed to answer a single question. All the others were jumping up and down to volunteer and shouting out answers to every question almost before it was asked. I don't think I made a very good first impression.'

Cassie and her mum were still grinning at Lauren's very accurate impersonation of Dr Joe and Lauren found herself smiling too.

'I'm sure tomorrow will be better,' said Sam.

'Everyone's different,' said Cassie, 'and Dr Joe knows that. I think by the end of the week he might be wishing he had more students like you.'

'Pick one thing that you loved about today,' said Sam. It was a game she played with her daughter when she'd had a bad day and it always made Cassie feel better.

'That's easy,' said Lauren, still smiling. 'Colin!'

'Ah yes, he's so gorgeous, isn't he?' said Cassie dreamily. 'Those big brown eyes . . .'

Her mother looked at her with a curious expression on her face. 'Who's Colin?' she asked, imagining an attractive young man.

'Colin the dog!' said Cassie.

Sam looked so relieved that Cassie and Lauren fell about laughing.

'I better go,' said Lauren, 'but thank you, both. You've really cheered me up. You're right, tomorrow will definitely be better. And I love your poster, Cassie! Where are you going to put it?'

'I hadn't really thought about it yet,' said Cassie. 'Mum's going to make copies. I guess at all the local shops, at school and at the park, of course.'

'How about I give you a hand putting them up tomorrow?' offered Lauren.

'That would be great, Lauren, thanks! I'll meet you at the clinic after school.'

Chapter Seven

By the time school finished the next day, Cassie had already put up six posters around the buildings. Everybody at school was already talking about it. Cassie's teacher, Miss Smith, had already said she'd be first in the queue on Saturday with her little Jack Russell, Rollo.

Cassie and Ben had just gone home long enough to drop off their schoolbags and pick up Ripper and Florence and then headed straight to the clinic. It was calmer today, and Margaret was clearly visible in her usual spot behind the reception desk.

'Hi Margaret, can we put one of our posters up in here?' asked Ben.

'Of course! In fact, Lauren told me all about it and rearranged the whole noticeboard to make room. See that big space in the middle? That's for you. And maybe put one in the window too, so that everyone can see it from outside,' said Margaret.

'Lauren has just popped out the back with Bill to walk one of the dogs, and I think Grace is keen to help! Dr Joe was so pleased that they're getting involved,' she continued.

Cassie busied herself with posters and tape. As was she standing back to admire her work, Lauren and Grace appeared; Lauren, again with Colin, and Grace, with an old black labrador called Penny. Both dogs looked very attractive in their bright blue singlets.

'Perfect timing!' said Cassie. 'Let's get down to work.'

By the time they unleashed the dogs at the park an hour later, every shop between the clinic and the park had a poster hanging proudly in the window. There was one on every fence post, gate and noticeboard within the park, and they already seemed to be attracting a lot of attention.

Ripper, as usual, led the way, running for the sheer pleasure of it, with Florence hard on his heels, bumbling along cheerfully. Penny seemed happy to stick close to Grace, enjoying the fresh air and the good company, while Colin, growing in confidence, had found a playful border collie puppy, who was quite happy to share his ball.

As they walked they chatted with whoever came their way. Everyone was talking about the charity dog-wash. It had created quite a buzz, and Cassie and Ben's excitement was growing with it; they could talk about nothing else!

'I think Penny's had enough,' said Grace as they were passing their gate for the fifth time. 'We might call it a day.'

'Yes, it's probably time for us to go too. Come on, Ripper!' called Cassie.

Ripper came bounding over and sat obediently while Cassie attached his lead. Florence came too, and Ben was convinced for a split second that she would follow Ripper's good example and let him put her lead on without the usual performance. She sat still until Ben got within an arm's length. Then she set off at a gallop into the centre of the park with Ben at her heels. She loved this game!

As Lauren, Grace and Cassie stood back to enjoy the show, they noticed an elderly woman nearby who they hadn't seen before. She had a Maltese terrier sitting beside her and it looked as though she was trying to coax the dog to its feet. But the terrier seemed quite distressed, and every time it tried to stand it looked really shaky and lay down again.

'Hey, is everything okay?' asked Cassie.

The lady was beginning to get very upset and answered Cassie in quick-fire Chinese. The only words that Cassie could understand were 'Bella, Bella,' but it was obvious that the lady was both very worried and that she spoke no English. Cassie was stumped, but it was clear that the dog was seriously hurt or ill. What could she do?

'Cassie, could you look after Colin for a moment?' asked Lauren, handing Colin's lead over to Cassie. Then she turned to the lady and started talking quickly and confidently to her in Cantonese.

The lady became calmer and more reassured now that she had found somebody with whom she could communicate. Lauren stepped forward and quickly examined the terrier where it lay on the ground before picking it up and cradling it to her chest.

'Let's get this dog to the clinic,' said Lauren.

She turned to the lady and, putting an arm round her shoulder, ushered her out of the park, talking calmly to her the whole time.

Chapter Eight

As they came through the door of the clinic, the other students sensed that something was wrong and crowded around asking questions, questions, questions!

Lauren pushed through and ignored them all, concentrating on the ill dog in her arms.

'Margaret, this is an emergency. We'll need Dr Joe as soon as possible,' she said firmly and continued through to the consulting room with Bella the Maltese and her owner.

The students stepped back at once to give her more space and couldn't help raising their eyebrows at her determined tone.

By the time Lauren laid Bella on the examining table, Dr Joe was there by her side.

'What's wrong?' he asked the owner, but she just stared blankly at him and shrugged her shoulders before looking back at Lauren. Lauren reassured her calmly in Cantonese that everything was okay. Dr Joe raised his eyebrows and smiled at Lauren, suitably impressed.

'This is Cynthia,' said Lauren. 'She's on holiday from China and is staying with her niece in Abbotts Hill. Bella is her niece's dog. They've already been down to the beach for a walk this morning, but it was only this afternoon at the dog park when she noticed that Bella was behaving strangely. She said she seemed disorientated and wobbly on her feet and her bark sounded different.'

All the time she was talking, with an encouraging nod from Dr Joe, Lauren was firmly feeling the dog all over. She had started right at the tip of her nose and spent a long time working her way back down Bella's face to her furry ears. She didn't miss a bit! Dr Joe, with his many years of experience, had already picked up on

Lauren's concerns and had started his search from the back, the very tip of Bella's tail, and was working his way forward.

'So you're thinking –' started Dr Joe as his hands continued searching.

'I'm thinking it must be a tick,' finished off Lauren. 'And judging by the severity of the symptoms, I think it's probably *Ixodes Holocyclus*, commonly known as the paralysis tick. Bella may have picked it up at the beach this morning.'

'I think you're right, Lauren. Pretty spot-on diagnosis,' said Dr Joe. 'Now, all we have to do is find that tick, pronto!'

Chapter Nine

It seemed like a long time later that Lauren gave a triumphant 'Aha!' and smiled at last.

Lauren and Dr Joe had searched the dog three times over and had just begun to consider the possibility that they may need to clip all her hair off to get a better look when suddenly, on the fourth look, Lauren found the horrible little tick stuck right in between two of Bella's tiny toes. It was no bigger than an apple pip!

Cynthia clapped her hands and smiled. No translation was needed to see the relief she felt.

Dr Joe carefully removed the tick with tweezers, popping it into a jar with a lid so that the other students could see it too. It was a useful thing to be able to identify, after all. The students and Cassie and Ben gathered at the door and breathed a collective sigh of relief, but Dr Joe and Lauren both appeared grave.

'It could be another day or two before there's any real improvement in Bella's condition, couldn't it, Dr Joe?' asked Lauren quietly.

'Yes,' replied Dr Joe. 'Bella is not out of the woods yet. Her symptoms could continue to get worse for another forty-eight hours before we see any improvement at all. The most important thing we can do now is keep her still and quiet.

'I'm going to give her this,' he said, filling a syringe. 'It's a mild sedative that will calm her down so that we can set up a drip for the anti-toxin. Then we'll find a quiet spot where we can keep a close eye on her. Will you bring Cynthia up to date? Let her know that she's welcome to visit, but it's unlikely Bella will be fit to go home for a few days yet.'

Lauren sat talking the whole thing over with Cynthia until her niece, Emily, arrived to take her home.

'Thank you so much,' said Emily. 'My poor aunt must have been very distressed. She can't believe her good fortune to have found someone in the dog park who could speak such perfect Cantonese!'

'My grandmother would be happy to hear you say that,' said Lauren modestly. 'My mum moved to Australia when she was just a little girl and completely forgot her Cantonese. So when I was born, my grandmother moved in with us to help look after me and she was determined that I should know my mother tongue. Granny is the only person I ever speak to in Cantonese, but it certainly came in handy today.'

'Handy for us, for sure!' said Emily.

Lauren was the hero of the hour. Once Emily and Cynthia had gone home, all the students wanted to know what had happened in the park and the consulting room. The tick was passed round in its little glass jar, and everyone marvelled at the tiny size of it compared to the huge problems it could cause.

Lauren was a bit embarrassed to find herself the centre of attention but pleased too when Dr Joe started enthusing about her calm and professional attitude, not to mention her hidden talents.

Chapter Ten

Saturday morning arrived at last and with it all the bustle of the fundraiser. Ben and Cassie had been at the park since eight o'clock, getting everything just right. They'd rustled up an old market gazebo from a neighbour and had managed to put it up so that they would be out of the hot sun while they washed. Two long hoses went left and right, away from the taps, and a bright yellow baby bath sat in between them. Dr Joe had donated two large bottles of doggy shampoo, and Ben and Cassie were not going home while there was even a drop left!

Around the gazebo and along the fence in either direction were strings of colourful bunting that had been left over from the Girl Guides cake sale and kindly donated by way of Sarah at school. Several school friends had also made cardboard posters, which were now hung along the fence at regular intervals. Ben and Cassie were feeling pretty proud of themselves. They really hadn't forgotten a thing!

By nine o'clock the dog park was filling up and there was Miss Smith, true to her word, rushing along, dragging a reluctant Jack Russell behind her.

'Morning, Cassie! Morning, Ben! This looks wonderful! Now, Rollo, be a good boy. Here you go, Ben,' she said, handing over Rollo's lead to Ben and a ten-dollar note to Cassie. 'The first of many, I'm sure,' she said.

The vet students turned up next with Bill, as well as two other shelter volunteers, each with a shelter dog in tow and a whole bunch of leaflets to hand out regarding both the cat and dog adoption programmes run by the shelter.

Lauren was to be the money collector for the day and Cassie proudly popped Mrs Smith's ten dollars into the tin.

With all the kerfuffle surrounding the

new arrivals, it was unclear how Ben came to be quite so wet and quite so red in the face while washing little Rollo, but gosh, that dog was shiny and clean at the end of it all.

Cassie, with a dog trainer's insight, had filled her pockets with little liver treats and surprisingly found that the dogs she washed were all pretty well behaved.

It seemed that every dog they knew came through the park that morning and plenty that neither of them had ever seen before: Maguire the ball-obsessed cattle dog, Levi the chihuahua – who was so tiny they only charged five dollars – was the first to experience the luxury of the bathtub, Spinner the Spaniel, Tommy and Tallulah the Aussie Terriers, Barney, Chewy, Dixie, Rex, Rosie, Cookie, Coco, Josie, Cara,

Pumpkin, Pixie, Molly, Yogi . . . The queue went on and on and on.

'Hey, Cassie, it looks like it's going really well,' said Ben's mum, Veronica. 'I've been in line for ages!'

'Oh, hi, Veronica, I didn't see you there. Are you ready for a bath, Florence?' asked Cassie, turning towards the big fluffy Old English sheepdog.

Ben looked up from washing a beautiful little staffy-cross called Milo and sat back on his heels. Florence HATED bath-time and he just had to see how badly this was going to go.

But Ben was a little disappointed. Florence sat still while Cassie soaked her all over with the hose. Florence looked utterly miserable once she was wet but stood calmly while Cassie rubbed on the shampoo and lathered her all over.

The suspense was killing Ben; he was expecting Florence to run for it at any minute. He could feel laughter bubbling up inside him as he dried off Milo and popped the money in the tin.

Cassie carefully rinsed Florence and finished off by giving her the liver treat. Ben was gutted and even Veronica was amazed.

Then, suddenly, as Veronica was thanking Cassie and handing over her money, Florence ran. The lead was yanked from Veronica's hand and Florence headed straight for the gate. Ben ran after her, pleased at least to be proved right about his own dog.

After the whole morning of washing, the grass was wet and a huge, muddy puddle had formed between the dog-wash area and the gate. Florence had clearly spotted it earlier because she headed straight for it and performed a perfect dive right into the puddle's centre. Mud shot out in every direction and Ben was coated in it from head to toe.

Florence's gorgeously clean, silver-and-white coat turned brown and slimy and she sighed in sheer contentment as she did the cockroach – wriggling on her back, legs in the air and clearly loving every minute of it.

By lunchtime the queue was dwindling and when Alex Bannerman turned up at the park with a big brown paper bag, Ben and Cassie realised they were starving. Lauren and Grace were only too happy to take over for half an hour while Ben and Cassie enjoyed the luxury of sitting down and feasting on toasted cheese and tomato sandwiches and the banana and chocolate smoothies that Alex had brought with him.

'I have dessert too!' said Alex as he rushed off back to the deli, only to return minutes later with a huge tray of perfectly iced cookies. All the cookies were in the shape of dogs and cats. 'You can have one each only,' he warned. 'And I will give some to the students and volunteers. Everyone else will have to pay a dollar! It is for a good cause, after all,' he said with a wink to Ben and Cassie.

As Ben and Cassie nibbled away happily, Alex sauntered up to the front of the queue to give Lauren and Grace a cookie for later. He had the tray raised high above his head, balanced perfectly on one hand as though he was in a fancy restaurant. Just as Alex reached the girls, Lauren finished washing Belvedere, a very highly strung giant poodle.

Cassie could see what was going to happen just seconds before it actually did. She jumped to her feet and yelled 'Dad!' but it was as though everything became slow-motion.

Belvedere leapt to his feet and his owner grabbed for his collar just as Alex came between the two of them with his tray held high.

The perfect pirouette that Alex performed won admiring glances from the queue of pet owners. Alex was desperate to save the tray of cookies but, ultimately, there was nowhere else to go – the yellow bathtub full of dog hair and cold soapy water welcomed Alex, bottom-first.

Cassie put her hands over her eyes and only removed them when seconds later a cheer went up from the queue, followed by loud applause. Her dad was sitting almost upright in the baby bathtub. He looked as if he might need a hand to get out . . . but the tray of cookies remained high above his head. Not one had dropped to the floor!

Chapter Eleven

It was at the end of an exhausting day, as Lauren and Cassie were taking down the bunting and Ben was dismantling the gazebo, that Cynthia and Emily walked past.

'Hello Lauren,' said Emily. 'Dr Joe said you would be here. We've just been to pick up Bella. She's made such an excellent recovery and it's all thanks to you!' Emily opened the pet carrier she was carrying to show them the sleepy-looking but healthy Bella inside.

'I don't think she's quite well enough to take a bath here yet. But the next time you have a dog-wash, we'll be first in line,' Emily said as she put enough money into Lauren's tin to pay for several baths.

Dr Joe was the next and last visitor. He ushered the students back to the clinic with the shelter dogs and the tired volunteers, with strict instructions to meet at the deli in twenty minutes.

The day had been an amazing success. Ben, Cassie and Lauren were counting the money as the other students entered the deli. Colin was curled lazily at Lauren's feet with no blue singlet to be seen! And Alex came round the counter and managed to put down a whole tray of milkshakes without any dance moves whatsoever.

Dr Joe stood up and looked down at the group of people stretched across the three tables that had been pushed together. All the students were there, as well as the volunteers and Ben and Cassie, Cassie's parents and his own wife, Veronica. He was so proud of everyone that he could hardly speak.

'Cassie,' he said, 'would you like to tell us how much money you and Ben have raised today?'

Cassie got to her feet, 'Drum roll, please,' she said.

Ben obliged, with his hands on the table top. 'The total is . . . one thousand and forty-two dollars!'

A cheer went up around the table.

'A wonderful achievement, you two,' he said to Ben and Cassie. 'But you know what is an even bigger achievement? You've raised awareness in Abbotts Hill about the plight of abandoned dogs, cats and, particularly, kittens.

'Today we received pledges from people in our own community to adopt every one of the new kittens when the time comes, as well as one of the mummy cats too. I know it's a relief to us all to know that they're going to wonderful homes where they will be loved.

'On top of that, we've had a lot of

interest in our shelter dogs. My wonderful students and volunteers have been out with the dogs every day this week and the knock-on effect is that we have re-homed seven of our long-term residents, as well as one recent arrival, who I know is going to be very happy to be going home with a new owner this evening.'

Lauren blushed before saying, 'Mum and Dad popped into the shelter today to see Colin, who I've been talking about all week. They fell in love with him too, and it just feels great to be able to offer him a new home. I think he'll love living with us.'

Colin would no doubt have agreed completely if he hadn't been snoring contentedly at her feet. It had been a busy day, after all.

'I've had such a wonderful week, Dr Joe,' continued Lauren. 'We've learnt so much.' The other students nodded in agreement. 'Thank you on behalf of all of us.'

'Thanks, Lauren, and to all of you. I wish you well in your careers. I know you'll all make terrific, caring vets in the future,' said Dr Joe. 'I've kept my favourite bit of news for the end,' he continued. 'And I know you'll like this, Cassie. Microchips work! Our lovely little mummy Peppermint has found her way home!

'Her owner contacted us today. Peppermint went missing from home after her family moved house nearly six months ago. They presumed she must have been run over by a car and had just about given up on ever finding her.

'They're going to pick her up in seven weeks, once her kittens are old enough to go to their new homes.

'They've agreed to have her de-sexed too so that there's no chance of the same thing happening again. It's such a good result all round! Well done, everyone!'

A yawning Cassie turned to an exhausted and dirt-covered Ben. 'Want to do it all again next weekend?'

Ben gave a small Florence-like whine as he rested his forehead on the table in front of him.

Cassie patted him on the back. 'What about the weekend after?'

ABOUT THE RSPCA

The RSPCA is the country's best known and most respected animal welfare organisation. The first RSPCA in Australia was formed in Victoria in 1871, and the organisation is now represented by RSPCAs in every state and territory.

The RSPCA's mission is to prevent cruelty to animals by actively promoting their care and protection. It is a not-for-profit charity that is firmly based in the Australian community, relying upon the support of individuals, businesses and organisations to survive and continue its vital work.

Every year, RSPCA shelters throughout Australia accept over 150,000 sick, injured or abandoned animals from the community. The RSPCA believes that every animal is entitled to the Five Freedoms:

Fact File

- freedom from hunger and thirst (ready access to fresh water and a healthy, balanced diet)
- freedom from discomfort, including accommodation in an appropriate environment that has shelter and a comfortable resting area
- freedom from pain, injury or disease through prevention or rapid diagnosis and providing veterinary treatment when required

- freedom to express normal behaviour, including sufficient space, proper facilities and company of the animal's own kind and
- freedom from fear and distress through conditions and treatment that avoid suffering.

RSPCA

TICK PARALYSIS PREVENTION FOR YOUR PET

Paralysis ticks (*Ixodes holocyclus*) are among the most dangerous parasites that can affect your pet.

The paralysis tick is found on the eastern seaboard of Australia, from North Queensland to Northern Victoria, particularly in bushland.

Fact File

How does the tick cause paralysis?
The tick sucks blood from the host animal
and secretes saliva that contains toxins.
These toxins enter the bloodstream and
cause poisoning.

How to identify the paralysis tick
They tend to be light blue to grey in
colour, ranging in size from two or three
millimetres to as large as 10 millimetres. But
even the smallest tick can cause paralysis.
Once on the animal, the tick embeds
itself firmly into the skin. When an adult
tick feeds on blood, it increases in size
dramatically.

Symptoms of tick paralysis
- Loss of coordination in the hind legs
- Change in voice or bark
- Retching, coughing or vomiting
- Loss of appetite
- Progressive paralysis to include the
forelegs
- Difficulty breathing or rapid breathing

Fact File

What to do if your pet shows symptoms of tick paralysis

1. Keep your pet calm and in a cool, dark place until you take it to the vet.
2. Do not offer food or water, as this may lead to pneumonia and breathing difficulties if your pet can't swallow properly.
3. Seek veterinary attention as soon as possible.

How to protect your pet from paralysis ticks

During the tick season, don't take your dog walking in bushy areas. Keep lawns and shrubs short and remove compost material from backyards.

Search pets every day for ticks: Use the fingertips to feel through the animal's coat. Ticks or tick craters can be felt as lumps on the skin surface.

Although most ticks are found around the head and neck of the animal as well as

Fact File

inside the ears, they can end up anywhere on the body. It is especially important to search long-haired dogs very thoroughly between the eyes and the end of the nose. The most reliable way to locate the ticks is to systematically run your fingers through your cat or dog's coat.

Once located, a tick hook is useful to help remove the tick. If the head is left in, the tick will die anyway and will no longer inject poison. Always assume there is more than one tick and continue your search.

A New Home
for Cocoa

Helen Kelly

RANDOM HOUSE AUSTRALIA

Chapter One

'Sophie, Sophie! Sophie Miller!' screeched Mr Harris, the Abbotts Hill School bandmaster, as he brought the students to a juddering halt for the third time in ten minutes. 'We don't need you to play with such vigour. While I love the trumpet, it might be nice to hear some of the other instruments too, don't you think?'

'Yes, Mr Harris, I'm sorry. I'll try to play more softly,' said Sophie.

'What's got into Sophie?' whispered Cassie Bannerman to her neighbour and firm friend Ben Stoppard. 'I don't think I've ever seen her get told off so many times before.'

'True,' said Ben. 'And she doesn't look particularly sorry either . . .'

The two of them glanced over at Sophie who, far from being embarrassed or put out, was grinning from ear to ear and appearing as though she could jump out of her seat at any minute.

Catching sight of Cassie looking at her, Sophie gave her a little wave. Cassie smiled back before being interrupted by

Mr Harris's baton, tap, tap, tapping on the music stand in front of him.

'Thank you, Mr Stoppard,' said Mr Harris, looking pointedly at Ben. 'Perhaps you could take this opportunity to reduce your volume too? Okay, let's take that one from the top!'

Ben and Cassie smirked at each other. Now that was more like it! Everyone was used to Ben being told to quieten down. He'd only joined the band when he'd moved to Abbotts Hill a term and a half ago. Mr Harris had tried him out on a few different instruments in those early weeks.

Ben was determined to be in the band but when it came to selecting an instrument, he'd proved a little picky. He'd lasted three weeks on the flute, but it was just too quiet

179

and, let's face it, *girly*. That tiny case looked like a handbag! And though the clarinet was slick, it was actually tricky to get the hang of; he'd lasted two weeks. But once Ben had settled on the bass guitar, the band was never quite the same.

Mr Harris had secretly hoped that Ben might tire of the bass in the same way he had with the previous instruments. But not this time. He'd stuck with it for ten long weeks so far.

The bass guitar had an amp with a volume dial that could go really loud! Ben, in the privacy of his own bedroom, had perfected the moves of the ultimate ROCK GOD! It was only a matter of time now before Mr Harris and the rest of the band would fully appreciate how utterly fantastic and musically talented he really was. It was in his blood!

The rest of the rehearsal went off more sedately, and by the end Mr Harris was back to his normal calm self.

'That's much better, Junior Band!' said Mr Harris as the children started to pack away their instruments. 'If we keep playing as well as that, I think we'll steal the show on Friday!'

Friday was going to be big. The mayor was coming to the Abbotts Hill Public School to officially open the new school hall, and the Junior Band had been asked to perform a few pieces as part of the occasion.

'Now, if I could have two volunteers – Ben, Sophie – to put the music stands away?' asked Mr Harris.

Ben and Sophie looked at each other and groaned. How was *that* volunteering?

'Oh, Cassie, before you go could I just have a quick word with you about your, um . . . your scales?' said Mr Harris, walking towards the door.

Cassie was a bit worried. She wasn't the best clarinet player in the band but she thought her scales were pretty good. She took a deep breath and followed him out into the playground, prepared for a 'pull your socks up' talk.

Chapter Two

'Ooh, Cassie's in trouble! Cassie's in trouble!' sang Ben as he and Sophie joined Cassie in the playground a few minutes later and they strolled together to the school gate.

'Yeah, right,' said Cassie. 'I must've been taking lessons from you.'

'So, what did he say then?' asked Ben.

'Nothing. He just thought I should practise my scales a bit more, that's all,' said Cassie, smiling to herself.

Ben looked a bit sceptical. Was Cassie up to something?

'But, Sophie!' Cassie exclaimed, changing the subject completely and turning to face her friend. 'What got into you? You looked just about ready to explode during rehearsal!'

'I'm getting a kitten today!' Sophie squealed with delight.

'Wow, no wonder you can't sit still. That's great!' said Cassie, giving her a hug.

'Yeah, I think if I was getting a new cat I'd play the trumpet loud enough to pop eardrums too,' joked Ben. 'It makes perfect sense now. You were trying out cat noises on the trumpet!'

Sophie and Cassie grinned and rolled their eyes.

'Cass, you know more about cats than anyone else I know. I was wondering if you would come with me?' asked Sophie.

'To get your kitten? I'd love to!' said Cassie, who was now almost as animated as Sophie. 'You know, Ben's dad works at the RSPCA shelter. He'll love that you're going to give one of their kittens a loving home!'

'The RSPCA?' said Sophie. 'No, Mum's taking me to the big pet shop at the mall. We saw the cutest little tabby on the weekend. I hope he's still there! Even Mum fell in love with him, and you know she's never been keen on getting a pet . . .'

In her enthusiasm Sophie failed to

notice the look that was passing between Ben and Cassie. Cassie's face had darkened and all her excitement had drained away. Ben's face was a picture of gleeful mischief.

This should be worth seeing, he thought. There was no way Cassie Bannerman would go into a pet shop to buy a cat when there were dozens of healthy and friendly abandoned cats and kittens at the RSPCA shelter, all desperately in need of a loving home.

But Cassie didn't have a chance to get another word out.

'There's Mum now,' said Sophie, watching a black car pull over to the kerb. 'You're going to love this kitten, Cassie! We can pick you up at about 5 o'clock, okay?'

'Okay,' said Cassie quietly. 'Umm . . . I'll see you then.'

Ben could contain himself no longer. As Mrs Miller drove away he burst out laughing. 'Cassie! Are you really going to go? I'm trying to imagine you in a pet shop. It's not going to end well . . .'

Cassie smiled, a determined look on her face. 'I don't think Sophie and her mum have really thought this through,' she said.

'Ah, I see now,' said Ben, adopting his mad-scientist voice. 'You're going to *manipulate their minds* into believing they really want to get a cat from the RSPCA and not the pet shop.'

'Exactly!' Cassie grinned.

'Mwa ha ha ha,' cackled Ben, rubbing

his hands together as they started walking home.

'Hey, maybe you could manipulate Mr Harris's mind too!' suggested Ben when they approached his house.

'Why? To make him believe you're the best bass guitarist Abbotts Hill has ever seen?' asked Cassie.

'Well, obviously it's only a matter of time before he discovers that for himself,' said Ben airily. 'But I think Friday's performance would be greatly improved by a bass guitar solo right in the middle. You know, where it goes duh na na duh...'

Ben threw his schoolbag and guitar case into the garden and started to demonstrate just how it should be.

He definitely had the posture right,

Cassie thought to herself as he strutted about with an invisible guitar, *but not very much else*.

Cassie glanced over the gate to see Florence with her paws over her head as though she was hiding.

The Old English sheepdog was clearly not a fan. Cassie could understand where she was coming from. Although, to be honest, the bass guitar noises that Ben was making with his mouth were actually a lot easier to listen to than when he played them on the guitar.

Cassie sidled through the gate and gave Florence a big rub on her chest.

'It's okay, Florence. I'm sure this will all blow over in a few days,' Cassie whispered to the shaggy dog, scratching her behind the ears. 'Let's see what we can do, shall we?

A little *mind manipulation* might not go to waste after all.' Cassie giggled to herself.

As she waved to Ben and turned to carry on home, she could see Florence dragging the abandoned guitar case by its handle, up the garden path. Ben, oblivious, played on to the adoring audience in his head.

Chapter Three

By the time Sophie, her mum and Cassie arrived at the pet shop that evening, Sophie was at bursting point. The whole way there Cassie had talked and talked about her cat Gladiator and the RSPCA as she tried to get Sophie and Mrs Miller to consider the possibility of getting a kitten from the shelter. But both seemed completely besotted with the tabby they'd seen on the weekend. It appeared that no other cat would do.

'We'll still be giving a cat a loving home, Cassie,' said Mrs Miller. 'Surely that's the important thing?'

Cassie smiled. 'Yes, but it means that there's one more cat in the shelter that won't get a home. The RSPCA doesn't make money from selling the cats. They just re-home those that have been abandoned; ones that otherwise might die.'

Mrs Miller looked as though she was about to say something in return when she was interrupted by her daughter's excited cries.

'Cassie, Cassie,' yelled Sophie. 'Here he is!'

Cassie and Mrs Miller went over to her, and within a few seconds the pet shop owner appeared too.

'Aw, he really is adorable, isn't he?' said Cassie, admiring the little tabby her friend was so intent on making her pet.

'He is,' said the shop owner, 'but I'm afraid he's sold. The new owners are collecting him in the morning,' he said, opening the cage. He picked out the tabby and gave him to Mrs Miller, who hugged him close.

Cassie noticed the disappointment on Mrs Miller's face. They caught each other's eyes before turning to Sophie, expecting tears at the very least.

Sophie shrugged. 'Mmm. What about this one, then?' She was pointing at an orange cat in the same cage. 'He's cute too! We could call him Marmalade. Or Pumpkin.'

The owner took the orange cat out to hand to Sophie, but she had disappeared off to the next cage, where she continued to coo over a new kitten.

Cassie took the orange kitten and tickled its soft, furry tummy.

'How old are they?' Cassie asked the owner.

'They're all between eight and ten weeks old,' he replied.

'Are any of them litter-mates? They all look so different,' mused Cassie.

'One or two might be, I guess,' said the shop owner vaguely. 'But we get them from a variety of breeders up and down the state, so . . .' He tapered off and Cassie got the

impression that he didn't really know much about the kittens, except how to sell them.

'How long do you keep them here for?' Cassie continued.

'Oh, these little cuties sell themselves, really. Everyone falls in love with them!' he said cheerfully. 'I've hardly ever had to send them back. Are you buying one?'

'No, it's just Sophie,' said Cassie, gesturing to her friend. 'My cat Gladiator is six years old. I got him from the RSPCA when he was as tiny as this little guy. His mum had been thrown out by her owner, even though she was expecting kittens!'

The owner looked at his watch, took the orange kitten from Cassie and popped him back into the cage. Mrs Miller put the tabby back in too.

'So which one is it going to be?' asked the owner, glancing at his watch again. He seemed keen to be getting on with other things.

'I think we need a little longer to decide,' said Mrs Miller.

'Sure thing,' he replied, returning to the sales desk.

'Mrs Miller,' said Cassie, 'at the RSPCA they take a lot of care to match you up with a cat or kitten that will fit in with your family. They don't just hand out cats to anybody.'

'You know, Cassie, I think you're right,' she said decisively. 'Sophie!' she called. Now that the tabby kitten was no longer available, Mrs Miller was starting to see things a bit more clearly.

Sophie scampered over from the back

of the shop, where she'd been falling in love with six other kittens.

'Mum, I just can't decide. I love them all!' Sophie exclaimed.

'I know, and I think that's just the problem,' said Mrs Miller. 'I think we're going about this all wrong. There's no hurry.'

Sophie looked crestfallen. 'So we're not getting a kitten today?' she asked.

'I'll tell you what,' said Mrs Miller, 'why don't we sit and think things over for a bit? There's an ice-cream stall over there, and I for one do all my best thinking in the company of a good Raspberry Ripple.'

Sophie and Cassie grinned at each other and shrugged. It was hard to argue with that kind of logic.

Chapter Four

'In summer the RSPCA is open late on Mondays,' said Cassie to no one in particular, as she polished off her mint choc-chip ice-cream.

'It is?' said Mrs Miller.

'Yes, for people who can't get there during the day. So it will be open now,' mused Cassie. 'And I bet it's not even that busy.'

'We better get a move on, then,' said Mrs Miller. 'Before it closes.'

'Really? Yay!' said Cassie as she and Sophie jumped to their feet. This mind manipulation thing really *was* working!

Entering the RSPCA shelter was very different to entering the pet shop, and never having had a pet before, neither Sophie nor her mum were really sure what to expect.

The vet clinic was open too, and Dr Joe and Margaret were both behind the reception desk when they walked in, and the waiting room was silent and empty for a change.

'Hi Cassie,' said Dr Joe as he came around to the front of the counter. 'What can I do for you this evening?'

'Hi Dr Joe, I've brought you some cat lovers,' said Cassie. 'This is Sophie Miller from school, and her mum,' said Cassie, politely introducing her friends. 'And this is Dr Joe Stoppard,' she said to Mrs Miller, 'otherwise known as Ben's dad.'

'Call me Mel,' said Mrs Miller as she shook Dr Joe's hand.

'Sophie's thinking about getting a kitten, Dr Joe. She's never had a pet before, and I thought you would be the best person to help her pick the right one,' said Cassie.

'Ah, well yes, you've certainly come to the right place!' said Dr Joe. 'We have no shortage of cats here. Why don't we go through to the cattery and I can answer some of your questions while you admire our friendly felines?'

'Sounds good,' said Cassie, while Mel and Sophie smiled their agreement.

Chapter Five

The 'cattery' was actually a large room with walls lined from floor to ceiling with cages that contained either a single cat or a family group of a mother cat and kittens. There were so many cats!

'So, have all these cats been abandoned?' asked Mel, hardly able to believe it.

'Many of them have,' said Dr Joe. 'But they're not all strays. There are plenty of reasons why they end up here. Some people surrender their pets to us because they are moving overseas or because they're sick and can't look after them. Often, people lose their job and feel they can't afford to keep a pet, or they move into a new apartment and find that pets aren't allowed.'

Sophie and Cassie were working their way down one side of the room, stopping every couple of seconds to look and admire.

'They're just so adorable, Cassie. I want to take them all home!' said Sophie, who had calmed down a good bit since the afternoon.

'Kittens are cute, Sophie,' said Cassie. 'But you have to remember that they don't stay like that for very long. By Christmas, that baby will be fully grown,' she said, pointing to the tiniest kitten. 'I think that's why lots of cats end up here. People think they'll have that cute kitten forever and then it grows up. Cats can live for upwards of 15 years, you know.'

'Wow!' said Sophie. 'So the kitten I get now will still be my cat when I'm . . . 23! Oh, look at this one, she's just gorgeous.'

'A little tortoiseshell – she's beautiful!' Cassie agreed.

She was still a kitten but older than most of the cats they'd seen. She stared back at them with wide eyes but seemed afraid and made no attempt to come closer.

'Why is she scared of us?' asked Sophie as Dr Joe and Mel caught up to them.

'She's not scared of you in particular,' said Dr Joe. 'She's just a bit anxious in general. Hannah has only been here a few days. She was abandoned by her owner and doesn't seem to have been treated very well.'

Dr Joe moved closer to Hannah's cage. 'It'll take her a little while to trust any human again, so we'll be doing some training with her for a few more weeks before she is ready to be adopted. And then we'll have to make sure she goes to someone who has time to spend with her; probably an older person who is home all day and has a quiet house with no other pets.'

'Is that why she's got an orange tag on her cage?' asked Cassie.

'That's right, Cass,' said Dr Joe. 'Did you notice that all the cats have a tag?'

206

Sophie looked around and saw that every cage had an orange, blue or green tag attached to them. 'What does the blue tag mean?' she asked.

'Well, I was just chatting to your mum about your house and I understand that you have two little sisters and a very busy household. Not to mention a bigger girl who enjoys playing the trumpet loudly.'

Sophie grinned and Dr Joe continued.

'So the cats with the blue tag would be just perfect for your family. It means that those cats love playing with children and don't mind noise and bustle. They're pretty affectionate too and will love being pampered by you and your sisters. They'll settle into your house and family with no trouble at all and, most importantly, each and every blue-tagged cat here prefers the trumpet to any other instrument in the whole band.'

'Dr Joe? Does the green tag mean that those cats like the bass guitar?' asked Cassie with a cheeky grin.

'Sadly, Cassie,' said Dr Joe with a grimace, 'there is no cat in the world that favours the bass guitar. And in fact, even dogs have been known to leave home and turn up here voluntarily when the amp is turned up too high.'

'Hey Sophie,' called Mel, who had wandered down the row a bit. 'What do you think of this little guy? His name's Cocoa and he seems like a perfect darling.'

Sophie took one look at the jet black cat with the white socks and fell instantly in love.

Chapter Six

On the way to the park with Ripper the next morning, Cassie decided to take a detour to Ben's house to see if he and Florence were going for a run before school. Ripper and Florence were close friends and often started their day with a bit of a rumble.

But as she approached the Stoppards' place, there was a terrible high-pitched squealing noise. They hurried up the path in alarm, Ripper barking with concern.

It wasn't until Cassie was standing at the front door that she recognised the sound.

It's Ben tuning up his bass guitar, thought Cassie with a smile.

But several minutes later Cassie realised he wasn't tuning it up at all – he was playing one of the songs that they'd been rehearsing at school for weeks. A song that was going to be performed before the mayor in just a few days!

'It's not going to be pretty, Ripper,' said Cassie, frowning.

Ripper agreed, dutifully sitting to attention on the doorstep. He stared worriedly up at Cassie with raised eyebrows, making her laugh as she rang the doorbell.

Ben's mum opened the front door, appearing bleary-eyed and rather cross. The raucous noise from upstairs got even louder.

'Morning, Cassie,' she said, drumming up a weak smile.

Before she could say another word there was a flurry of activity as Florence pelted down the stairs and out past Cassie, almost bowling her over! Even Ripper was taken aback at the low growl coming from his usually mild-mannered friend. Florence stopped at the gate, where she lay as flat as she could with her paws over her face. She was not happy.

'Poor Florence. She doesn't like music, then?' asked Cassie innocently.

'I think she's just ready for a run,' said Mrs Stoppard as she and Cassie shared a knowing look.

'So the mind manipulation worked?' said Ben when they arrived at the dog park.

'Yes! Sophie's very pleased,' said Cassie. 'She picked a black kitten called Cocoa. Your dad gave them all the paperwork to fill in at home and lots of leaflets about caring for your cat. They're hoping to pick him up this evening. She's so excited!'

'That's great. Hopefully her mind will be back on her trumpet before the performance on Friday,' said Ben without a hint of sarcasm.

'Yes,' said Cassie, a little uncertainly. 'It'd be so embarrassing to be noticed for all the wrong reasons, wouldn't it? By the mayor, of all people?'

'Yeah, but she'll be fine now, you'll see. We'll sound awesome!' said Ben as he started a game of football with Florence and Ripper.

Cassie didn't know what to think. Could Ben really not know what an awful bass player he was? Couldn't he hear himself playing? Couldn't he see the effect that his playing had on every single human being and animal that had heard him?

She wasn't too sure what to do. There was no way Ben could play the bass on

Friday! And she wasn't convinced her mind manipulation skills would do the trick this time.

Chapter Seven

'Hi Cassie,' sang Sophie as she entered the Bannermans' deli that evening.

Cassie was finishing up some chores for her mum, putting box after box of crackers on the shelf, and was quite ready to have an excuse to stop for a little while. Her dad, Alex, had baked some of the deli's popular biscuits for an order that day, and their sweet buttery scent wafted in the air.

'Hi Sophie. Are you on your way to pick up Cocoa?' she asked.

'We have him already!' she squeaked, and right on cue Sophie's parents walked through the door with her two little sisters and a pet carrier in tow.

'Wow, you didn't waste any time,' said Sam, Cassie's mum, as she came from the back of the shop to check out the Millers' new feline arrival.

'He's adorable,' continued Sam. 'Do you remember when we brought Gladiator home, Cass? He was no bigger than that, and look at him now. He's part of the furniture.'

'You know, Sam, the whole process was just so straightforward. We just wanted to pop in and thank Cassie for all her advice,' said Mel, placing the carrier on the floor. Cocoa was fast asleep, snuggled up in a fleecy blanket.

Gladiator, hearing his name and thinking it might mean food, appeared out of nowhere. Seeing no food, he had a lazy full-body stretch and gave the pet carrier a reasonably thorough sniff. Then he went back to his warm spot in the front window where the sun was coming through.

'Dr Joe has been great,' said Mel. 'Cocoa has already been desexed and microchipped. He has also had his vaccinations as well as a full health check, so there's nothing left for us to do except take care of him. I think he's going to fit in beautifully. Isn't he, girls?'

219

Molly and Zoe, Sophie's younger sisters, nodded shyly. Sophie beamed.

'Anyway, we should be heading home to get this little boy settled in,' said Mel.

'It doesn't seem as if you're going to get a cuddle from him today, Cassie,' said Sophie, looking down at the sleeping kitten.

'But why don't you and Ben come home with Sophie after band practice tomorrow and you can have a proper introduction?' said Mel.

'I'd love to, and I'm sure Ben will too!' replied Cassie enthusiastically.

Chapter Eight

'Sophie, Sophie, Sophie!' groaned Mr Harris the next afternoon at band practice, as he once again brought the band to a grinding halt.

Cassie and Ben swapped an amused look.

'What now?' whispered Cassie.

'Everything sounded fine to me,' Ben said, shrugging.

Yes, well everything would sound fine to Ben, thought Cassie. *He probably couldn't hear a single other instrument in the hall since his amp was turned up so loud!*

'You need to put a bit more into it!' said Mr Harris. 'I can't hear you at all today and you're allowing the flutes to drown you out. Can you manage a bit more oomph?' he asked.

'Yes, sir, I'll try,' said Sophie quietly before being overcome by a huge yawn.

The whole band giggled, and Mr Harris tapped his baton on the music stand to quieten them down again.

'I hope we're not keeping you up, Miss Miller!' said Mr Harris. 'Although I don't know how anyone could fall asleep in the same room as Mr Stoppard. Ben, could you please take this opportunity to turn down your volume? Thank you, let's continue.'

Ben grinned and turned the dial on his amp. Cassie smiled over at Sophie, hoping to make her feel better but Sophie didn't even notice. She was too busy yawning.

'I could hardly keep my eyes open in there!' moaned Sophie as she, Cassie and Ben walked towards the gate. 'I didn't sleep till late last night because I was playing with Cocoa. I've made a nice and cosy place for him to sleep, in a basket next to my bed.

Then I woke up early this morning just so he wouldn't feel too alone. Poor thing, I couldn't bear to think of him being by himself for the entire night.'

'You must be exhausted,' consoled Cassie. 'I remember Gladiator taking a few nights to settle in at first. Do you know what really helped?'

'What?' said Sophie.

'One of these!' said Cassie, taking out a perfectly wrapped gift from her bag and handing it to her friend. 'I should have given it to you yesterday.'

Sophie carefully unwrapped the parcel. 'A teddy bear?'

'You'll see,' said Cassie. 'They love to snuggle up with something warm. I guess it must make them feel as if their nice warm mummy is right there beside them.'

'Thanks, Cassie. Anything is worth a go,' said Sophie, giving Cassie a hug.

By the time the trio reached Sophie's house, Cassie and Ben were very excited about meeting Cocoa. But as soon as Sophie opened the back door and stepped into the kitchen they could tell that something was wrong.

The room was in chaos! Molly was on all fours under the table looking for something. Little Zoe was going through the kitchen cupboards with the concentration of a forensic scientist, and Sophie's mum was out in the hallway searching the cupboard under the stairs. She'd almost emptied it, and boxes of old paper, jars, clothes and sports equipment were scattered around.

'Mum?' said Sophie. 'Is everything all right?'

Mel pulled her head out of the cupboard and her sisters jumped up in surprise. They looked at Sophie worriedly.

'What is it?' asked Sophie as Zoe sniffled and started to cry.

'I didn't mean to,' wailed Zoe.

'What's the matter, Zo-Zo? What happened?' asked Sophie.

'Cocoa's gone missing,' said Mel with a grimace.

Chapter Nine

'But how could he have got lost?' said Sophie, close to tears. 'Dr Joe said he should stay in the smallest room of the house for a week or two until he gets used to his surroundings. How could he get out of the laundry?'

Zoe's crying got louder. 'I just wanted to play!' she bawled.

'One thing we can be certain of,' said Mel, 'is that he couldn't have got out. The back door was closed and we'd already gone round and shut all the windows. So wherever he is, we'll find him!'

'Okay,' said Sophie with renewed determination. 'Let's go!'

Within seconds Cassie, Sophie, Molly and Mel had scattered to the furthest reaches of the house to find Cocoa. Ben, having never been in the Miller place before, felt a little uncomfortable rummaging around in it, so he stayed put in the kitchen, where his only company was the teary Zoe.

'It'll be all right, I'm sure they'll find him,' said Ben in what he thought was a very consoling voice. But small crying people were definitely not Ben's area of expertise and the little girl continued to cry as loudly as ever.

Ben didn't know what to do, but felt he should be doing something! Bewildered, Ben and Zoe continued to stare at each other until Zoe eventually said, 'What's that?'

Ben looked at the guitar case he was holding. He had been too distracted by the household's hullabaloo to have thought of putting down his instrument. 'This is my bass guitar. I play it in the band with Sophie and Cass. It's pretty cool! Have you ever seen one?' said Ben, eagerly hoping that Zoe's interest in his guitar might cheer her up.

He took the shiny red guitar out of its case and he thought Zoe looked suitably impressed. Her tears were definitely starting to slow down.

'Shall I play you a tune?' asked Ben

Zoe nodded silently.

Ben's eyes drifted to a pair of small music speakers that were on the kitchen bench. 'It will sound much better with some power behind it,' he said, deftly plugging in the guitar cord to the speakers.

The guitar filled the small kitchen with such a violently raucous, twanging, clanging noise that Zoe's tears dried up very quickly indeed. The child was wide-eyed and speechless. Within seconds Cassie, Sophie, Molly and Mel came running into the kitchen to see what on earth was happening.

Ben was in his element. With his back to the door he didn't realise that his audience had expanded. Nor did he

hear or see the tiny, black, squawking flurry of fur that launched itself from the middle shelf of the open pantry and across the room into the safety of Sophie's arms.

'Cocoa!' cried Sophie.

Ben played on, oblivious to the fact that Zoe had started to cry again. Cassie eventually took the matter into her own hands and tapped Ben gently on the shoulder.

As he turned to face Cassie the noise came to an abrupt stop. There was a few seconds of shocked silence as the audience removed their hands from their ears.

Ben finally spotted Cocoa back in Sophie's arms, and before he had a chance to say anything, Zoe stepped up and yelled at the top of her voice, 'You're too noisy!

232

You scared our Cocoa!' before flouncing out of the room.

'Hey, I helped you find him!' said Ben. 'You should be thanking me!'

Chapter Ten

The school hall's official opening ceremony was on the next day.

Parents and visitors filed into the hall and took their seats while the band set up their instruments and music stands for the first big performance of the year.

The students seemed calm and pre-pared; they'd practised hard, and Mr Harris had been so proud of them in their last rehearsal before the show. Both Sophie and Cocoa had had a really good night's sleep thanks to Cassie's teddy bear, so there would be no falling asleep on the job today!

Ben, on the other hand, was running round like a headless chook.

'Cassie, I can't find my guitar lead! I know it was in the bag with my music!' cried Ben.

'Ooh I hope you didn't leave it at Sophie's house! Isn't there a spare one in the cupboard?' said Cassie.

'There usually is, but I can't find that either. Mr Harris is going to blow a fuse!

And there's Mum and Dad coming in now,' said Ben, completely beside himself.

His parents waved to him before taking their seats in the front row, right next to the Bannermans. 'They've both taken the afternoon off work to see me. This is my first ever public performance. And I'm not even going to be able to play!'

'Leave it to me,' said Cassie, and she went over to speak to Mr Harris.

Ben was cringing in his seat, but within minutes Cassie came back beaming.

Mr Harris beckoned Ben over to the store cupboard. 'Ben, I understand you're missing a vital piece of equipment?'

'Yes, sir, I'm really sorry.'

'No matter, because I've realised that what we really need is a very specialised percussionist. I'd hate for you to miss out on today, and I think with your terrific sense of rhythm, you'd really bring a lot of flair and natural talent to this instrument,' said Mr Harris.

Ben was feeling better already. He hadn't realised that Mr Harris had recognised his musical genius. He nodded in agreement.

'There aren't many people I could ask at such short notice, you know. You will have to pay close attention to your music and watch for my cue, okay? You'll be centre stage! All eyes will be on you.'

'I know I can do it, Mr Harris,' Ben replied, feeling terribly important.

As the mayor took his seat, the lights went up and the band launched into their first tune. Cassie could see Dr Joe and Veronica Stoppard scanning the band for a sight of their son. She smiled reassuringly at them and then found that she couldn't stop smiling at all. She loved it when a plan came together! Mind manipulation indeed . . .

As the final tune came to its glittering climax, with the music building up and up, Ben walked confidently onto centre stage and, with his eyes firmly on Mr Harris's baton, raised his arms.

As the tune reached its final bars Mr Harris made three tiny twitches of his baton in Ben's direction. Ben raised the enormous cymbals and CLASH! CLASH! CLASH!

The audience rose to their feet and applauded wildly while the ears of Ben and all those around him were still ringing.

Ben took a bow and looked thrilled. His very own solo!

'You were awesome, Ben!' said Cassie as they were putting the equipment away after the performance.

'You know, I think percussion may be my thing!' said Ben, still glowing from the applause. 'Mr Harris thinks I might be a natural on the cymbals. The bass was good, but those cymbals are seriously loud! The only downside is that I won't be able to bring them home to practise.'

'Ah well, you can't have everything,' Cassie said and shrugged. She stacked the last couple of stands and went to put them away.

'Thanks, Cassie,' said Mr Harris, coming over to her. 'I really don't think I could have done it without you,' he said, giving her a high five.

As Cassie walked away, she glanced back and shared a smile with Mr Harris as he took the guitar lead out of his jacket pocket and put it away in the cupboard.

Chapter Eleven

'He's just gorgeous!' gushed Cassie, gently rubbing Cocoa's soft little tummy. 'He's so fluffy and cuddly!'

Sophie and Cassie were sitting on the Millers' kitchen floor, appreciating the blissful silence that could only exist in a room that didn't have Ben and his bass guitar in it. Cocoa was the star attraction, and after the excitement of the past few days, Cassie had been looking forward to a proper play with him.

The silence was short-lived, though, as Mel came in the back door with Molly and Zoe, all rosy-cheeked from the garden. The girls joined Sophie and Cassie in a circle on the floor, and Cocoa went from girl to girl, collecting hugs, tickles and cuddles.

'He has fitted right in with us, Cassie,' said Mel. 'I'm so glad that the tabby cat had been sold! We would never have thought of getting a kitten from the RSPCA, and it feels so right to have given a home to a cat that really needs it.'

'He's definitely landed on his feet in this home,' Cassie agreed.

'And thanks too for the teddy bear. It did the trick perfectly; I don't think he'll ever sleep without it again!' said Mel as she prepared afternoon tea on the table.

'If he's anything like Gladiator, he'll move on to a larger model pretty quickly!' said Cassie. 'Gladiator loves snuggling up to me and he keeps my feet warm on cold nights.'

Giggling erupted from the circle of girls as Zoe lay flat on the floor, while Cocoa took an experimental walkabout on her. Zoe could hardly breathe she was laughing so hard, and Cocoa wisely jumped over into Cassie's lap.

'Well, I ordered a special afternoon tea surprise to thank you for your great advice and help,' said Mel. The girls jumped up to sit at the table.

'Yay! Cocoa cookies!' yelled Molly and Zoe.

'And lemonade! Yum!' added Sophie.

'I think I've seen biscuits like these before,' said Cassie, admiring the gorgeous cat-shaped cookies.

Each one was perfectly iced in black and frosted with white little socks. The tip of each tail was white too, and the eyes were dotted a brilliant blue.

She took a bite. 'Gosh, you know I've tasted biscuits like this before too,' said Cassie, grinning widely.

Mel's eyes twinkled but she gave away nothing.

'Dad really does make the best biscuits ever, doesn't he!' said Cassie, laughing.

ABOUT THE RSPCA

The RSPCA is the country's best known and most respected animal welfare organisation. The first RSPCA in Australia was formed in Victoria in 1871, and the organisation is now represented by RSPCAs in every state and territory.

The RSPCA's mission is to prevent cruelty to animals by actively promoting their care and protection. It is a not-for-profit charity that is firmly based in the Australian community, relying upon the support of individuals, businesses and organisations to survive and continue its vital work.

Every year, RSPCA shelters throughout Australia accept over 150,000 sick, injured or abandoned animals from the community.

The RSPCA believes that every animal is entitled to the Five Freedoms:

Fact File

- freedom from hunger and thirst (ready access to fresh water and a healthy, balanced diet)
- freedom from discomfort, including accommodation in an appropriate environment that has shelter and a comfortable resting area
- freedom from pain, injury or disease through prevention or rapid diagnosis and providing veterinary treatment when required
- freedom to express normal behaviour, including sufficient space, proper facilities

 and company of the animal's own kind and

- freedom from fear and distress through conditions and treatment that avoid suffering.

CARING FOR YOUR NEW KITTEN

There is nothing as curious, playful or as energetic as a young kitten. To keep kittens in top health, they need special care.

Diet
Attention to your kitten's diet is very important. You will find it easy to feed your kitten correctly if you observe a few simple rules. Naturally, a kitten is best fed a balanced diet to ensure he or she receives all the necessary nutrients from a young age.

Basic kitten feeding guide:

• Ensure your kitten has a balanced diet. Talk to your vet directly for advice.

Fact File

- Provide high-quality premium commercial kitten food that is balanced and appropriate for your kitten's life stage and health status.

- Regularly provide moist foods in the diet, e.g. high-quality wet canned kitten food.

- Provide access to grass (avoid chemically treated grass and toxic plants) – kittens will sometimes eat grass, which may be a source of vegetable matter and micronutrients.

- Kittens should be offered food at least four times a day.

- Ensure fresh drinking water is available at all times.

Fact File

- Do **not** feed the following (note: this list is not exhaustive): onions, garlic, chocolate, coffee or caffeine products, bread dough, avocado, grapes, raisins, sultanas, currants, nuts, including macadamia nuts, fruit stones (pits).

- Do **not** feed fresh meat and offal (e.g. liver) only, as that does not constitute a balanced diet and can lead to serious nutritional deficiencies.

- Be aware that some pet food products, such as pet meat/pet mince/processed pet rolls, can contain preservatives that will make kittens very sick or even kill them. Talk to your vet for further advice.

- You may also offer some human-grade fresh raw meaty bones occasionally to provide some variety, e.g. raw chicken wing or raw chicken neck occasionally to help keep teeth and gums healthy. Safety tips for raw meaty bones include:

  - *Bones must be raw and they must be human-grade.*

Fact File

- Always check with your vet first whether raw bones are suitable for your particular kitten.
- Raw bones should be introduced gradually. The bone must be large enough so that the kitten cannot fit the whole bone in its mouth.
- Too many raw bones can cause constipation. One raw bone per week is generally well-tolerated.
- Always supervise when your kitten eats raw bones. Avoid large marrow bones, large knuckle bones or bones sawn lengthwise as cats may crack their teeth on these.
- **Never** feed cooked bones as these may splinter and cause internal damage or become an intestinal obstruction.

Fact File

Worms

Kittens can be seriously affected with worms without any obvious signs of disease showing. However, the kitten will eventually become quite ill and can easily die if a worm infestation is left untreated.

Talk to your vet about worming and which products are safe to use for kittens and cats. Generally, kittens should be wormed every fortnight until three months of age, monthly until six months of age and then every three months for the rest of their lives.

You can buy either tablets or pastes to worm your kitten, but ensure that the drugs you are using kill tapeworms as well as

Fact File

roundworms and hookworms. Two separate medications may sometimes be necessary to achieve this.

If your cat or kitten commonly eats insects, lizards or other small animals, it may become infected with an uncommon tapeworm called a spirometra. This worm is not easy to kill. Presently there is only one medication that will successfully remove it. To be certain products are suitable and safe, buy worming medications from your veterinarian.

In addition to intestinal worms, cats may also be infected with heartworm — just like our canine companions. Discuss the best options for your kitten with your local vet.

Fact File

Vaccination

Kittens also need to be vaccinated. Here is an example of a kitten vaccination schedule:

- The first vaccination at six to eight weeks of age for temporary vaccination against feline enteritis and cat flu.

- The second vaccination at 12 weeks of age for the same diseases.
- Your kitten may then receive a third vaccination at 16 weeks of age. Thereafter, the cat may require a vaccination once a year or once every three years depending on the circumstances, but talk to your vet first as they will be able to advise further.

Fact File

It is also possible to vaccinate your pet against other infectious and potentially fatal diseases that have a lower incidence in our cat population. Discuss this with your local vet.

Fact File

Fleas

Talk to your vet about how to safely prevent and treat flea infestation. Check with your vet which product is best to use, to ensure it is safe for your feline.

Caution is needed when tackling fleas in cats because cats are very susceptible to insecticide toxicity. **Never use dog products on cats or kittens (because dog products can kill them).** Please be sure to read the label to confirm that it is a safe preparation for cats and that you are using it at the recommended dilution.

Fact File

Desexing
The RSPCA believes that all cats should be desexed. This is for the benefit of the cat in question and also for the benefit of the general cat population.

If mated accidentally, a cat will produce unwanted kittens, which often suffer by being introduced into a world where they will find difficulty in securing a home. There is a serious oversupply of cats and kittens, leading to many unwanted and homeless kittens and cats in Australia.

The RSPCA practises early-age desexing from the age of eight weeks, when the

Fact File

surgery is simple and the recovery is fast. If your cat was not desexed prior to sale, they should be desexed before they are able to produce any unintended litters.

There is no benefit in letting your cat have a litter first. In fact it is very important to prevent litters to try to reduce the number of unwanted kittens and cats.

Fact File

Microchipping

It is very important to ensure your pet kitten or cat is microchipped because if your pet becomes lost, you are far more likely to be reunited with your feline. Also make sure that your family's contact details are recorded against your cat's microchip number on the microchip register, as this will help with identification.

For more information visit the **RSPCA Australia knowledgebase** (kb.rspca.org.au)

Florence Takes the Lead

David Harding

RANDOM HOUSE AUSTRALIA

Chapter One

Ben Stoppard's mum turned off the lights and started singing 'Happy Birthday' as the twinkling candles on the cake she was holding came into view. Ben joined in the song. His dad blew out the candles with a grin before hugging Mum.

This was unbearable. There were still seven whole months until Ben's birthday. Watching someone else celebrate was really hard, especially when it was his dad. He always got such boring presents!

Ben sighed and stood up. Seeing his parents embracing in the dim light made this the perfect time to flick on the light switch. He reached for it, only to trip over Florence, his shaggy Old English sheepdog, who had been dozing beside his chair.

'Florence!' grunted Ben as his palms fell against the wall, stopping his fall. 'You're always in the wrong place at the wrong time!'

Ben's parents unlinked their arms just as the light came on. Florence turned her neck and looked up at Ben with glassy eyes. Immediately he felt sorry for snapping at her. After all, Florence was his best friend – along with Cassie, who lived up the road.

'Thanks, guys,' said Ben's dad, sitting down again. 'The cake looks delicious, Veronica!'

'So,' said Veronica, 'who wants a really big piece?'

Both Ben and his dad raised their hands as Florence barked loudly from under the table.

Ben laughed. 'Sorry, girl, chocolate's no good for dogs!' he said, passing Veronica the cake knife from across the table.

'It isn't that good for people either,' said Ben's dad, patting his stomach.

Now it was his mum's turn to laugh. 'Oh, Joe!' she chuckled as she licked icing off her fingers. 'I think it's probably time for presents. I want to leave mine until last. How about yours, Ben?'

Ben wolfed down a mouthful of cake and slid a small gift across the table. 'Sorry, it's not much,' he said. 'I couldn't think of what to get you.'

'Well, I like the gift wrap. That's a good start.'

Ben had wrapped the present in paper covered with cute dogs wearing sunglasses. He thought his dad, who worked as a vet at the RSPCA, would appreciate that. The card matched the paper. 'It's your birthday . . . *so why not have a hot dog?*' read Dr Joe, who began to laugh. Ben smiled.

The present was a mug for his dad to use at work and a key ring. 'Oh, thanks, Ben, my old key ring broke just a few days ago!'

As Dr Joe hugged him, Veronica gave Ben a secret wink. The key ring had been her idea. 'Okay, my present now,' she said, full of excitement.

Ben's dad unwrapped her gift to find a brand new touch-screen mobile phone. 'Wow,' he said. 'I wasn't expecting this! I hope I can use it – technology really isn't my thing.'

'I'll show you how,' said Veronica, who was glad to have had time to buy her husband's gift during her lunch break at work. She was a doctor at the local hospital and often worked long hours. 'It's got lots of great features and it will be more reliable than your old one.'

'True,' Ben's dad admitted.

'Plus,' she continued, 'I thought we could give Ben your old phone. We could get him a prepaid account and then he can use it to call home in an emergency.'

Ben was excited. He had never owned a mobile before. Maybe his dad having a birthday wasn't as bad as he had thought.

'But I have one more surprise for you, dear,' said Veronica, 'and I think you'll love it!'

Chapter Two

The next day at school was a hot one. Ben couldn't wait to tell Cassie about his mum's surprise. As soon as the lunch bell rang, Ben met Cassie under the shade of the massive tree at the top of the playground's grass area. They both sat down and waved themselves with paper fans that Cassie had made during art class.

'Phew,' said Ben, 'I haven't been this sweaty since the cross-country race.'

Cassie laughed, remembering her victory. 'What about that time we ran around Abbotts Park with Craig and his greyhound?'

'Oh yeah,' said Ben. He blushed as he recalled how much he had huffed and puffed that day.

'Well, we don't need to run anywhere today,' said Cassie. 'I'm happy in the shade. I hope Mum has put extra water out for Ripper and Gladiator.'

Ben smiled. 'Don't you ever stop thinking about your pets?' he asked.

'Ha ha, no!' said Cassie. 'You know how much I love animals.'

Ben did know. He was sure she would end up working as a vet for the RSPCA like his dad did. Secretly, he thought being a vet sounded like a great job, too.

'So how was your dad's birthday?' asked Cassie.

'Oh, I've something to tell you,' said Ben, sitting up straight.

'What?'

'For a present, Mum gave Dad a new phone so I get to keep his old one.'

'Cool,' said Cassie.

'And she surprised Dad by deciding to take the long weekend off working at the hospital – we're going away on holiday!'

Ben was ecstatic. His parents worked so hard at their jobs that he couldn't even remember their last family vacation. He couldn't wait to spend three whole days with both parents and no threat of them doing a night shift or being called into work for an emergency.

'Nice!' said Cassie. 'Where are you going?'

'Some small country town called Bunyan,' said Ben. 'It sounds a bit boring – I'll be taking a huge stack of comics – but it will be nice hanging out with Mum, Dad and Florence.'

'Bunyan?' repeated Cassie. 'We stayed near there once. It's big farm country. Do you think your dad will get to do some farm inspections while he's there?' Cassie still remembered the time Dr Joe took them both on a farm inspection and they ended up having to help bring a new foal into the world.

'No, this is strictly a holiday,' said Ben. 'Mum made Dad promise – *no work allowed!*'

'That's a shame,' sighed Cassie. 'Think of all the things he could get done for the RSPCA out there! He could check in with farmers working under the Approved Farming Scheme, offer a door-to-door veterinary service, promote higher-welfare farming at farmers' meetings, or –'

Ben laughed. 'Cassie, I promise that if anything turns up I'll ring you, okay? But to tell you the truth, I'm sure we'll all just end up lazing around and doing nothing. This heat is intense!'

Chapter Three

Ben couldn't wait for the long weekend to come. Three days without school! He spent Tuesday and Wednesday afternoons planning what he would take to entertain himself while his parents looked at all the boring arts and crafts shops you find in small towns. He also made sure that

Florence got plenty of time with Cassie and Ripper at the park. Ben knew spending three days without her best pal would be tough on Florence, and besides, he might miss Cassie too.

On Thursday afternoon, however, Ben slunk into Cassie's family deli, his shoulders drooping. Florence, looking just as demoralised, plodded in on her leash.

Cassie was doing some homework on a stool behind the counter as her mum sold a customer one tub of their famous bolognaise sauce.

Cassie's mum saw them first. 'Oh, hi Ben,' she said, giving the customer her change. 'What's up?'

'Nothing, Sam,' he grunted.

Cassie looked up from her work and

lowered her eyebrows. 'Hmm . . . I think this calls for a chocolate milkshake special,' she said to her mother.

Samantha Bannerman nodded and got to work on the drinks while Cassie and Ben sat down at one of the little tables. Florence barked happily as Ripper joined them from behind the counter.

Ben sighed. 'Mum said the holiday is off.'

'What?! Why?' asked Cassie.

Sam delivered two tall, frosty milkshakes with chocolate sprinkles and whipped cream on top.

'She said she can't find a guesthouse that allows pets,' said Ben, taking his first sip. 'And we can't just leave Florence at home. Besides, I don't want to go without her.'

Ben rubbed Florence's shaggy head and she barked twice in agreement.

'Hang on a minute,' said Cassie. 'I told you we've stayed in Bunyan before. Do you think I would've gone anywhere without Ripper?'

'What do you mean?' said Ben.

'Of course!' added Sam. 'We stayed at a lovely place. It's a little further out of town, but they allow dogs. Ripper loved it. I'll ring your mum right now and give her the details!'

Ben's face brightened. 'Gee, thanks!'

'Miss Webb, who runs the place, is really nice,' added Cassie, loudly sucking up the last of her shake. 'She even has her own little free-range chicken farm.'

DOG

The next afternoon, Ben's family were strapped into the station wagon with Florence safely travelling in the back.

Ben spent the two-hour ride reading and talking to Florence through the grille in the backseat. Halfway to Bunyan they let Florence out at a rest stop for a walk on her leash and some water.

They pulled up at the guesthouse just as it was beginning to get dark. An older lady, who Ben assumed was Miss Webb, waved from the front garden as the car's wheels crunched upon the gravel drive.

'This must be the place,' said Dr Joe, opening his door.

'And you must be the Stoppards!' said Miss Webb. She took off her gardening gloves and came to shake hands with Ben's parents.

Florence barked loudly as Ben opened the rear door and connected the leash to her collar.

'What a lovely dog,' said Miss Webb, her blue eyes crinkling. 'If you would like to get her some exercise before your dinner, we have lots of room at the back of the house. Feel free!'

'Okay, thanks,' said Ben.

'But keep her away from the chickens,' said Dr Joe. 'They shouldn't mix.'

'Oh, you've heard about my chickens, have you?' asked Miss Webb.

'Yes, and we can't wait for some free-range eggs with our brekkie tomorrow,' said Veronica.

Miss Webb laughed. 'They do say the only things happier than my hens are my guests after eating one of my breakfasts!'

Ben jogged around to the back field with Florence barking happily beside him. They found a water dish that Florence took a few big gulps from. It was just as hot here as it was back in Abbotts Hill.

It was very quiet in the country. Somewhere, Ben could hear hens clucking but that was it. And the sky was so clear too. It was still early, but he could see so many more stars than he could at home.

Ben smiled as he trotted around in the grass after Florence. He wondered what Cassie was doing back home, and he had no doubt in his mind that his friend would love it out here.

After a few minutes however, Ben noticed something else. A strange, low snorting sound was being carried on the warm breeze from somewhere in the distance.

Ben knew Florence could hear it too, but he had absolutely no idea what it was.

Chapter Four

Ben soon forgot about the strange noise when he returned to the guesthouse, a satisfied Florence in tow. After an evening of board games, the Stoppards slept late the next morning. Ben's mum said it was her first sleep-in all year.

Miss Webb's breakfast was as tasty as she had said it would be. Ben was given a plate piled up with scrambled eggs, bacon, tomato, mushrooms, sausages and beans, while rows of warm toast called to him from a rack in the centre of the table.

By the time Miss Webb came into the dining room to offer his mum and dad their second cups of coffee, Ben was slumped back in his chair.

'Ugh . . . I can't remember the last time I ate that much,' he said.

'I'm glad you liked it,' said Miss Webb. 'All the vegetables were fresh from the garden, and the eggs were laid by my chickens just this morning.'

'They're delicious,' said Dr Joe. 'Happy and healthy hens sure lay yummy eggs!'

'So what's on the agenda for today?' Miss Webb asked as she began to clear away the plates.

'I'd like to visit the arts and crafts bazaar we passed on the way here,' said Veronica.

'Oh yes, they have lovely things there,' said Miss Webb. Ben stifled a groan.

'I'd just like to take a nap out in the back porch first,' said Dr Joe, 'especially after that meal.'

'What would you like to do, Ben?' Veronica asked.

'Anything,' he said, 'as long as I get to run around with Florence a bit. I don't want her to feel left out.'

'Oh, don't worry about Florence,' said Miss Webb. 'I've just fed her a healthy breakfast out the back. She's having a snooze in the sun right now.'

The Stoppards looked at each other and smiled. Ben thought it was nice to meet someone who was happy to look after the entire family, not just its human members.

After the (very boring) arts and crafts shopping, Ben and his parents had a picnic lunch of milkshakes and freshly baked meat pies in town. Then they returned to the guesthouse to relax.

Sitting in a deckchair for a few hours didn't sound very thrilling to Ben, so he took Florence to the back field with her favourite frisbee.

'Ready?' he asked, tossing the disc up high.

Florence ran after it, looking upwards to gauge when and where the yellow frisbee would land. She jumped up at just the right moment with her jaws open and . . . dropped it.

'Never mind, girl,' affirmed Ben. 'Bring it back!'

Florence happily returned the frisbee for another throw. Ben was hoping to return to Abbotts Hill with Florence able to catch frisbees at least as well as Ripper already could.

Ben threw the frisbee again, but this time Florence didn't even move. Her ears were pricked up and still. Ben froze too. Then he heard it – the same muffled snuffling that they'd heard the night before.

'What *is* that?' he asked.

Suddenly Florence pounced. She barked loudly and jumped around as though she was on a trampoline.

'Florence! What's up?' called Ben.

He attached her leash and tried to calm her down, but she kept leaping around and dragging Ben towards some bushes. As they approached, a small and frightened rabbit shot out from under the leaves and ran off.

Florence growled and howled, trying to pull Ben towards it. She hadn't been listening to the strange sounds – she had been tracking the rabbit!

'Girl, settle down!' encouraged Ben, calling her back towards the guesthouse. After a short hesitation she gave up and trotted back as if nothing had happened.

Chapter Five

Ben needed a rest. After his dad offered to take Florence for a jog, Ben gladly agreed. He moped around his bedroom and the dining room before collapsing into a sofa in the lounge room.

Eventually, Miss Webb walked through from the kitchen. 'Hello Ben,' she said.

'What have you been up to?'

'First, Florence was going crazy out the back, trying to catch a rabbit,' said Ben. 'Now, I'm just bored, I guess.'

'Yes, we do have a lot of rabbits around,' said Miss Webb. 'When the early European settlers introduced them here I'm sure they weren't thinking ahead.'

Ben reached for a stack of magazines lying on a little table nearby. Titles such as *House & Home* and *Golf Pro* didn't exactly take his fancy.

Miss Webb smiled kindly. 'You know, when I feel bored or lonely, I always enjoy calling a friend on the phone and just having a good old chat.'

Ben's eyes opened. He'd forgotten all about his new phone. He didn't think calling Cassie exactly counted as an emergency, but he was dying to talk to her.

Miss Webb patted him gently on the shoulder before going back to the kitchen. Ben sped into his room and closed the door behind him. He found his mobile in his backpack and flopped on his bed.

Soon the dial tone was replaced by a friendly voice. 'Hello?'

'Cassie!'

'Yes, who's this?'

Ben laughed. 'You know who it is!'

'Ha ha, sorry,' Cassie chuckled. 'How's the trip going?'

'It's a pretty nice place,' said Ben. 'Really quiet.' A familiar barking sound came back at him through the speaker.

'Hello Ripper,' answered Ben. 'Florence misses you.' Ripper barked again before Cassie's voice returned.

'Ripper says to say hi to Florence for him,' said Cassie.

Ben smiled and said he would. He was feeling better already. Miss Webb had been right.

'Have you had any animal adventures yet?' asked Cassie.

'Not really,' said Ben. 'Although Florence did try to chase a rabbit.'

Ripper barked again.

Ben heard his dad jog past the bedroom window with Florence. He sighed. 'I should probably go,' he said. 'I'm only supposed to use this phone in an emergency.'

'Okay, have fun,' said Cassie.

'By the way, what do you think this sound is?' Ben tried to imitate the low, grumbling snorting sound that he had heard twice now from the back of the guesthouse. It was an odd noise and it didn't come out of his mouth quite right.

'Oh my goodness!' shrieked Cassie. 'That sounds like bubbling ooze rolling down a mountain.' She laughed. 'Or like there's something wrong with the drains at the deli again!'

Both Ben and Cassie howled with laughter. Ben thought for the hundredth time how lucky he was to have her as a friend.

Chapter Six

That evening, Ben's parents had decided they should all go to one of the quaint country restaurants in Bunyan. Before leaving, Ben took Florence out for a walk.

They walked once around the entire field. For the first time Ben saw Miss Webb's free-range chickens in the neighbouring yard. They had lots of space to peck around in and a large house for laying eggs inside.

'Now, don't worry about tonight, Florence,' said Ben. 'Miss Webb will give you dinner, and she said you can sit inside with her while she watches TV. We won't be long, anyway.'

Florence yapped in approval.

'Oh, and I almost forgot!' added Ben. 'I called Cassie. Ripper says hi.'

Florence's body stood rigid and she barked excitedly.

'Yes, I know, you miss your friend Ripper, don't y–'

But Florence was off, bounding through the grass, causing a couple of rabbits to jump away into the nearby bushland.

'Florence!' called Ben. 'Come back now!'

But Florence took little notice. She was having too much fun chasing those small, funny animals with the floppy ears.

'Woof! Woof!'

'Florence!' he called again, but she paid no attention.

Ben was really angry with himself. He should have learned from Florence's earlier adventure that she shouldn't have been without her leash. The open countryside wasn't exactly the same as the dog-friendly park back home.

It was now beginning to grow dark and Florence was nowhere to be seen. She had run off so fast! Then Ben heard her barking in the distance.

He ran the way he thought she'd gone, carefully pushing aside some branches as he found his way through the trees. *Why can't Florence come back when she's called!* Ben wondered.

He stopped. He hadn't noticed it before now, but the strange, snuffling groan was back, louder this time. Whatever it was, Ben was getting closer to it. For a moment he forgot about Florence and strode faster, anxious to see what was on the other side of the bushes.

A possum skittered up a tree trunk as Ben passed by. He could see a clearing now, and a wire fence. The weird noise was growing even louder. Ben realised that what he thought was one long groan was actually made up of hundreds of snorts and grunts mixing together.

And then there was another sound. A creature was howling. Its wail shook Ben like an earthquake.

'That's Florence,' he shouted, 'and something is definitely wrong!'

Chapter Seven

Ben ran. Hearing his dog crying out to him was horrible. He followed the fence around the property. Florence's howl was getting closer but Ben still couldn't see her.

And then, in the gloom, he finally spotted her. She was sitting up, twenty metres or so away, on the other side of the fence. She was howling in front of a large building that looked like a kind of brick barn.

Thankfully she didn't seem injured in any way.

'*Pssst!* Florence!' Ben hissed. 'What's wrong? Come back.'

Florence stopped wailing and looked at Ben. She panted at him, wanting him to come over the fence towards her.

'I can't go in there,' whispered Ben. 'And you shouldn't be in there either.'

The gruffly, snuffling noises were louder than ever now. Whatever was making them were inside the building. Every now and then, a squeal could be heard amongst the other sounds.

He looked up at the building's dark wall,

which sat just on the other side of the fence. Despite the warm evening, Ben shivered.

'I'm not following you in there,' said Ben. 'You have to learn to come when I call you!' He kept calling his pet, but she wouldn't budge.

It was when Florence lifted her head to howl again that Ben decided to try his firm voice. '*Florence!* Come here, now!'

The shaggy sheepdog lowered her head and crept reluctantly back to Ben on the other side of the fence. He gave her a good scratch behind the ears.

'Good girl,' he said, shocked that Florence had actually obeyed one of his commands. 'What's got into you?'

Florence turned towards the wall of the building that ran alongside the fence.

Ben knew that she wanted him to go inside.

Something important is in there, but what?

For the millionth time, Ben wished that dogs could talk. He always thought Florence could sense things he couldn't.

The unsettling noises were very loud now and definitely coming from inside the building. Ben's stomach grumbled. It was getting late and this was a mystery he did not want to solve.

Ben wished he'd brought his mobile to call Cassie. Surely this counted as an emergency. He didn't know what to do and she certainly would have.

'Come on, Florence, Mum and Dad will be waiting.'

Florence didn't move. She walked over and scratched at the wall.

'Okay,' sighed Ben. 'I'll take a quick look inside, but you stay here.'

Florence barked once and sat still. Again, Ben could not believe she was actually following his orders. He looked up at the wall and saw a small window. A branch, connected to a tree that grew nearby, stretched past it. He knew he shouldn't be on someone else's property, but it wouldn't be too hard to climb up and take a peek inside.

Ben propped himself up onto the thick, low branch and got his head level to the window. *Just one quick look,* he said to himself, *and then we can go and have a lovely dinner.*

He leaned towards the window as far as he could. The window had narrow gaps, and a strong smell came out of them, hitting Ben's face like a hot wall of steam. Ben pulled away before holding his breath and leaning closer again.

The snorting noises floated out as Ben peered into the darkness.

What in the world . . . ?

What Ben saw made him jump off the branch and run back through the field towards the guesthouse with Florence yapping at his heels.

Chapter Eight

Even though Ben had only peered inside the pig shed for a matter of seconds, it had felt like hours. It'd been hard to see much in the growing darkness. A small lightbulb had shone down from the building's ceiling, showing him the immediate surroundings through the window.

Ben had seen large sows – female pigs – lying on the concrete floor within stalls made of steel bars. The stalls were very small.

If the pigs he could see stood up, there would not have been enough room for them to take more than one step, or to turn around. Every pig he saw, however, was lying down. Some of them had feet sticking into neighbouring stalls as their backs pressed against the bars.

Ben had seen some little piglets too, struggling for milk from their mother's belly. A few piglets were in a separate section to their mother, still connected but given a bit of extra room so they couldn't be squished by their large mums.

But despite all of that, the things that

worried Ben the most had been the smell and the filth of the place. It was very dirty. Food troughs ran alongside where the pigs were lying. The pigs were covered in brown splotches from whatever they were lying in, and the heat mixed with the smell, making it an unbearable place for Ben to stay near.

And most troubling of all, Ben had only been able to see three or four pigs, yet he knew that rows and rows of them must have been packed inside that building, lying and snorting in the dark.

Ben looked down at Florence as they ran. He wondered, not for the first time, why so many people didn't seem to want to treat animals with respect. Guiltily, he remembered how impatient he had been with Florence just moments before. Now he knew she had been only trying to help.

As they approached the guesthouse, Ben saw Miss Webb's chicken yard. There were no chickens around. He figured they had all entered the hen house to sleep and had chosen to go inside for the night. Ben frowned. Those pigs he had seen had had no choice in what they did or where they lived.

'Oh, there you are, Ben,' said Veronica when he stepped inside. 'We were looking for you. Ready for dinner?'

Ben nodded. He wanted to get as far away from that pig farm as he could. He delivered Florence to Miss Webb and gave her a big goodbye pat.

'Don't worry, she'll be fine here with me,' said Miss Webb.

Ben let out a crooked smile, glad it was the truth.

Chapter Nine

Ben was very quiet over dinner and went straight to his bedroom when they returned to the guesthouse. Florence lay down next to the bed as Ben took out his mobile and dialled Cassie's number.

'Hello?' said Cassie.

Florence yapped at the sound of her best friend's owner through the phone and Ripper could be heard happily yapping in response.

For a moment Ben didn't say anything. Then he told Cassie all about the pig farm he and Florence had stumbled upon. When he had finished, it was Cassie's turn to be speechless.

Eventually she sighed. 'That's just . . . *disgusting*,' she said. 'I can't believe pig farmers are still using sow stalls.'

'Sow stalls?' repeated Ben. 'Is that what they call the small spaces the pigs were locked up in?'

'Yeah,' said Cassie, 'and the ones where the piglets are in a pen next to their mothers are called farrowing crates. In some other countries it is illegal to use sow stalls and farrowing crates.'

'They were terrible,' said Ben morosely. 'The pigs could hardly move – they didn't even have room to turn around.'

'Thanks to organisations like the RSPCA, sow stalls are being phased out slowly but they still exist, and at the moment there are no plans to phase out farrowing crates. It's especially sad because pigs are very smart animals,' explained Cassie.

'They are?' asked Ben.

'Yes! They have complicated social structures and need space to forage. And mother pigs need to use stuff like straw to build a nest for their piglets. I reckon they must be going crazy in there.'

Ben's feeling of shock was slowly replaced by anger. 'But why?' he gasped. 'Is it just so we can fatten the pigs and get more meat from them?'

'Maybe. I think some farmers believe that keeping pigs in confined spaces protects them from hurting themselves and other pigs,' replied Cassie.

'Even if that were true, don't pigs – any animals – deserve to be treated better than that?'

'Yes,' said Cassie. 'I think so. But not everyone agrees with us.'

'Dad!' said Ben, an idea forming in his head. 'He could go in there with his RSPCA identification badge and shut the farm down and free all the pigs!'

'Um . . . I don't think it happens like that, Ben,' said Cassie dubiously. 'People can't just shut down a farm if it isn't doing anything illegal.'

Ben groaned.

'But you're right. It would be good if an RSPCA Inspector could take a look just to make sure that they are at least not breaking the law. And maybe your dad could tell them about the RSPCA's Approved Farming Scheme standards.'

Ben smiled. He was always amazed at how much Cassie knew about animals and the RSPCA.

'So what can we do?' asked Ben. 'There isn't much time. We're leaving for home tomorrow afternoon.'

'I'm not sure,' said Cassie, 'but if I think of something, I'll ask Mum if I can message you on her mobile.'

'Okay, thanks,' said Ben. 'I'll talk to you soon.'

'Bye,' said Cassie as Florence barked her own farewell into the phone. 'And goodbye to you too, Florence,' she added. 'You're a good dog. Without you, we wouldn't even know about the pigs!'

'Woof! Woof!' Florence replied, taking pride in Cassie's parting words.

Ben pressed the button that ended the phone call and lay back on his pillow, one hand on Florence's head.

Cassie had been right. Without Florence, the pigs would never have been found, but he still felt helpless and didn't know what to do. Ben was glad he had talked to Cassie, but he wasn't entirely sure it had made him feel any better.

Chapter Ten

Ben couldn't sleep. It was a warm night, but that wasn't the problem. He couldn't get the pigs or their tiny stalls out of his head. Every hour or so he would roll over and check the time on the clock near the bed.

The night crept on slowly. At 6 am his mobile buzzed. Ben sat up straight and reached for his phone. It was a message from Cassie!

CANT SLEEP. U SHOULD TELL YOUR DAD ABOUT FARM. SURELY HE CAN CHECK THE PIGS ARENT BEING TREATED CRUELLY? :(

Ben sighed. It was right to tell his dad. Besides, he hadn't come up with any better ideas. He showered, got dressed and walked out to the breakfast table, where his mum and dad had just sat down.

'Hi Ben,' said Veronica. 'Are you feeling as refreshed as us? It's a good thing you're up early. We have a lot to fit in before we go home.'

Ben looked down glumly at the massive plate of food Miss Webb had placed in front of him. He poked at the eggs with his fork before reaching out for a slice of toast.

'What's wrong,' asked Dr Joe, wolfing down his sunny-side-up eggs. 'Still full from yesterday's breakfast?'

'Not really,' said Ben. He stared at the crispy bacon on his plate. It had been delicious yesterday, but now . . .

'Miss Webb, where did this bacon come from?' Ben suddenly asked.

'The bacon?' repeated Miss Webb. 'All my ingredients are home-grown or bought from outdoor-bred farms where the sows and growing pigs can forage for food, root in the dirt, play in straw and do all those other things that pigs like to do. I'm a big believer in eating right.'

'You mean there are free-range pig farms where the pigs go outside?' asked Ben.

'Of course. But they don't have to be free range. A big shed filled with straw that allows in plenty of light and fresh air and gives pigs lots of space – that's just as good,' explained Miss Webb. 'They're hard to find, but they're out there.'

Dr Joe put down his knife and fork. 'Ben, what's up?'

Ben told the others about following Florence to the pig farm. His dad's jaw dropped. His mum and Miss Webb just shook their heads in silence.

When the story had finished, Dr Joe turned to his wife.

Veronica gave her husband's arm a squeeze. 'I know you weren't meant to work during our mini-break, but this seems important.'

'I'm going to have to contact the RSPCA so we can get an inspector to pay a visit,' Dr Joe replied. It was the first time during their holiday that Ben had seen his dad look so serious.

Veronica nodded in agreement. 'I'd only be happy leaving this place knowing that we at least did something to help.'

Ben grinned and took a big bite from his toast. It was finally time to take action. 'So what we will do?' he asked. 'Call for backup? Swing in from a chandelier and bust the place?'

'No, Ben,' said Dr Joe gravely. 'This is something that has to be done by the book.'

Chapter Eleven

Immediately after breakfast, Ben's dad got in touch with the town's local RSPCA Inspector, George, who was more than happy to call by the neighbouring farm.

When George arrived, Dr Joe said that he, Ben and Florence would escort him next door. 'Besides, I'm sure Florence would love one last run in the countryside before we head back home,' said Dr Joe.

So the group drove the short trip around to the front of the property next door. The dirt road that led there was bumpy and dusty.

'Farms can be so out of the way,' said Ben. 'If it wasn't for Florence, no one would have known about this place.'

Florence barked from the back at the sound of her name.

'You've got quite a dog there. It will be interesting to see exactly what's going on,' George remarked, looking at Ben and Florence in his rear-view mirror.

By the time George was knocking on the farmhouse door, Ben was really nervous. He wished Cassie was here with him. Who knew how the farmer would react to this visit?

After a moment, a smiling, middle-aged man opened the door.

George explained who he was. 'I know this visit is unannounced,' he added, 'but I'd like to take a look around your farming property if you don't mind.'

'No worries,' the farmer said. 'I'm more than happy for you to do that.'

Just as Dr Joe, Ben and Florence were about to say their goodbyes and leave George to do the inspection, the farmer called out. 'They're welcome to have a look around too. I've got nothing to hide. You'll find no ill treatment of animals here,' he said.

Ben looked at Florence, who tilted her head. Florence had started this mission and Ben felt obligated to see it completed. He turned to his dad. 'Can we?'

Dr Joe frowned slightly. 'As long you don't mind, George, and you're sure you're okay with this, Mr . . . ?'

'Call me Rick,' the farmer replied. 'And it's not a problem at all. I'd be pleased to show you around.'

Florence was not thrilled about being tied up and left under a tree, but Ben patted her and promised they wouldn't be long.

As Rick took them through his property, Ben soon realised this wasn't a large farm compared to some of the other ones he had visited with his dad.

There were only a few outbuildings,

all identical to the one Ben had found the night before. Ben wasn't sure which one he had already seen the inside of, but he figured it didn't matter. The sounds coming from each building suggested they were all full of pigs.

Rick led them to one of the pig houses and opened the door. The same sounds and smells came out to meet Ben as from the night before. Though the light was better in the late morning sun, it certainly didn't help to make anything *look* better. The same scene was taking place – pigs lying in muck, barely able to move, as piglets suckled here and there.

Ben rushed his hand to his nose, but his dad and George didn't flinch.

'Rows and rows of sows,' said Rick. 'None injured, all fine examples of good breeding and farming practice. These girls make me lots of money at market.'

Ben wanted to shout out in anger, but he bit his tongue.

George spent a little while inspecting the stalls and examining the pigs. By the time he came back to stand with Rick, Ben and Dr Joe, he had a list of things to talk about.

'There is nothing illegal here, but . . .' George said with a small frown.

'Then what's the matter?' asked Rick, hands on hips.

'I think that Dr Joe might be able to suggest a better way of housing your animals,' George said, turning to Dr Joe.

'I know you care about your pigs. But tell me, why do you keep them in these conditions?' Dr Joe asked Rick.

'The sow stalls and farrowing crates, you mean?' said Rick. He let out a deep sigh and threw up his hands. 'It's just how it's always been done. Stalls stop the sows from fighting with each other for territory. Crates protect the piglets from being crushed as the mother lies down.'

Ben couldn't hold it in any longer. 'But would you like being kept in a box?' he asked. 'Surely you want your pigs to be happy and able to live a natural life?'

Dr Joe shot his son a warning look as if to say, 'Don't be rude to the farmer', but Ben felt that something had to be done.

'What do you mean?' said Rick. 'They're just pigs.'

'Pigs are very smart animals,' explained Dr Joe. 'Believe me; they have such complex social structures that they should not live out their lives in stalls. Also, they are foragers and need adequate space to snuffle for food and wallow in mud. That can't happen in these conditions. And there is no straw here for the mothers to build nests.'

Rick looked stunned. All four stood silently for a while just looking at the pigs. One large sow tried to stand up but soon gave up and lay down again in its confined stall.

They finally left the pig house and walked slowly back to the front of the property. Florence yapped happily, tail wagging, when Ben came into view.

Then Rick broke the awkward silence. 'I dunno,' he said, 'I get what you're saying, but it seems like a lot of time, effort and money to change something that works.'

'Maybe it isn't working as well as it seems,' said Ben. He untied Florence and she jumped around him, overjoyed to be released from the tree. 'Steady, girl!' Ben said. 'Sorry, she gets excited easily.'

Rick sighed. 'My animals aren't anywhere near as happy as that!'

After a while he turned to Dr Joe, shrugging his shoulders. 'I see your point – there's no reason why my pigs shouldn't be better looked after, but what can I do?'

Immediately, Ben remembered their conversation with Miss Webb that morning. 'The pigs can be bred outdoors!' he said as Florence barked in agreement.

Rick smiled and rubbed his chin. 'An outdoor-bred pig farm? Hmm . . .'

Chapter Twelve

After George had said his goodbyes, Dr Joe had offered to take Rick around to Miss Webb's property to show him her free-range egg plot.

'I'm telling you, Miss Webb,' said Rick, tapping his head, 'the wheels in this brain are turning!'

Miss Webb laughed. She had been taking her neighbour around her farm and talking about how and why she had set it up.

'Please, call me Charlotte,' she said, giggling.

'I have so much unused space on my property,' said Rick, 'it won't be long before I have a yard for my pigs up and running.'

'That's great,' said Ben.

'Well, it's certainly worth a try,' Rick added.

'I think your customers *and* your pigs will appreciate it,' said Dr Joe, grinning.

Before Ben knew it he was packed and sitting securely in the backseat of the station wagon, waving goodbye to Miss Webb.

As the car turned to leave, Veronica sounded the car's horn. *Beep-beep!*

'Woof, woof!' echoed Florence.

'Ow! Florence, that was right in my ear!' Ben cried.

'Now, don't get too annoyed at our Florence,' Dr Joe remarked, laughing. 'If it wasn't for her being her usual self and running off, we would never have been able to meet Rick or help his pigs.'

'True,' said Ben, rubbing his ear. 'I guess I should follow her lead more often.'

'Even if she is a bit cheeky sometimes,' chuckled Veronica.

Ben pulled his mobile out of his pocket. After returning from Rick's farm he had called Cassie again to tell her all that had happened. Somehow he had used up almost all of his phone credit in one weekend!

At first, Ben had missed having Cassie by his side to help out with the pigs, but he felt he had done all right in the end. He smiled to think how much he had changed since meeting the girl from the local deli.

Ben texted her one last time:

WE R ON OUR WAY HOME. AS HAPPY AS 4 PIGS IN MUD!

Less than a minute later, Cassie's response came back:

SEE U SOON! OINK OINK! :)

Ben couldn't help laughing.

'What's so funny?' asked Dr Joe.

'Oh . . . nothing,' said Ben.

Dr Joe looked at Ben's smile then to the phone his son was holding. 'Hang on,' he said. 'Have you been using your mobile to talk to Cassie?'

Ben blushed. He had been caught.

'If you're so good at using mobiles,' said Veronica, 'maybe you could help your dad with his. He can't make head or tail out of it.'

Now it was Dr Joe's turn to blush.

'Gee, Dad,' Ben said, laughing, 'even Florence could use a mobile.'

'Woof, woof!' agreed Florence heartily. She had always known she was the smartest dog in the world. Now everyone else was starting to see it too.

RSPCA

ABOUT THE RSPCA

The RSPCA is the country's best known and most respected animal welfare organisation. The first RSPCA in Australia was formed in Victoria in 1871, and the organisation is now represented by RSPCAs in every state and territory.

The RSPCA's mission is to prevent cruelty to animals by actively promoting their care and protection. It is a not-for-profit charity that is firmly based in the Australian community, relying upon the support of individuals, businesses and organisations to survive and continue its vital work.

Every year, RSPCA shelters throughout Australia accept over 150,000 sick, injured or abandoned animals from the community. The RSPCA believes that every animal is entitled to the Five Freedoms:

Fact File

- freedom from hunger and thirst (ready access to fresh water and a healthy, balanced diet)
- freedom from discomfort, including accommodation in an appropriate environment that has shelter and a comfortable resting area
- freedom from pain, injury or disease through prevention or rapid diagnosis and providing veterinary treatment when required

- freedom to express normal behaviour, including sufficient space, proper facilities and company of the animal's own kind

and

- freedom from fear and distress through conditions and treatment that avoid suffering.

PIG FARMING

- The biggest welfare problem facing Australian pigs at present is the intensive confinement of sows (female breeding pigs) in narrow stalls and farrowing crates where they cannot move around easily.

- Pigs that are housed in sow stalls and farrowing crates have no opportunity to engage in exploratory and foraging behaviour, or to interact socially with other pigs.

- In November 2010, the Australian pork industry announced it would voluntarily phase out the use of sow stalls by 2017.

- In May 2012, the Tasmanian Government announced it would be fast-tracking the phase out of sow stalls, thereby sending a strong signal to other Australian states that intensive confinement of animals is no longer acceptable.

Fact File

- The next step for the industry will be to stop using farrowing crates — these are similar to sow stalls and confine the sow just prior to giving birth, during birth (called 'farrowing') and while she is nursing her piglets. The farrowing crate prevents the sow from carrying out key behaviours, such as seeking a nesting site and building a nest for her piglets.

- Animal welfare groups, including the RSPCA, believe that pregnant sows can be successfully housed in groups, provided that they are properly managed and have sufficient space to avoid aggressive encounters.

- Alternatives to sow stalls include straw yards with individual or electronic feeders to regulate food intake. There are also alternatives to farrowing crates. These include farrowing pens, which provide bedding and allow more movement, and extensive systems that use individual huts for farrowing.

RSPCA

Animal Tales

RSPCA

Animal

AVAILABLE NOW

Tales

COLLECT THEM ALL

THERE'S SO MUCH MORE AT
RANDOMHOUSE.COM.AU/KIDS